# ARDABIOLA

# ARDABIOLA

A Fantasy by

## YEVGENY YEVTUSHENKO
*Translated by Armorer Wason*

St. Martin's Press
New York

Library of Congress Cataloging in Publication Data

Yevtushenko, Yevgeny Aleksandrovich, 1933–
  Ardabiola.

  I. Title.
PG3476.E96A88   1985         891.73′44         85-2557
ISBN 0-312-04823-8

First published in Great Britain by Granada Publishing.

First U.S. Edition

10 9 8 7 6 5 4 3 2 1

# ARDABIOLA

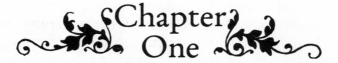

# Chapter One

The girl could feel someone watching her. She was wearing a cap – not some leather Parisian affair but an ordinary woolly one – and she thought the stare was directed at her cap, rather than at herself. She was already pretty fed up with being looked at, sometimes with curiosity, sometimes with disapproval, but maybe she went on wearing the cap precisely to spite people staring at her. Some looks merely slip over you as if they've got no substance, but this one had weight to it, making the girl almost flinch.

She was standing on the rear platform of a jam-packed old tram, pressed against the window so that the peak of her cap came up against the glass. A fat man in a Ukrainian embroidered shirt with red tassels had placed a full-length oval mirror, which he had only just managed to squeeze into the tram, on her cheap velveteen shoe. It was in a frame of imitation bronze scrolls, made to resemble Winter Place furniture or something of the sort. The Artists' Workshop label still dangled from the back of it. The girl had barely got her foot free and had drawn it up as there was nowhere to put it. The fat man's face was reflected in the mirror to the left of the girl, his eyes bulging under a huge purple growth on his forehead, which made him look like a rhinoceros. Grasping the mirror with the vast arms of a wrestler, he fixed it with a savage gaze. Who would win, he or the mirror, had yet to be decided. Two glazed eyes of indefinite colour, half-shaded by a greasy, shapeless hat, swayed on the girl's right. A hiccup came from under the hat by the girl's shoulder, enveloping her in a fruity smell of cheap alcohol. The bottle occupying her neighbour's pocket dug painfully into her hip.

The stare the girl felt did not come from inside the tram. She looked out of the window and saw that it was from the driver of an orange Zhigulenka estate car which had almost collided into the tram's bumper. Some boys had created a musical diversion by attaching an empty tin can to the bumper and it bounced along the cobbles to the movement of the tram. The windscreen of the car was dusty and the driver's face only half visible, but his eyes could be seen distinctly, as if they had an existence separate from his face. They were like two unnaturally blue shiny balloons, suspended in mid-air over the steering wheel of an empty car, which moved along of its own accord without a driver. The girl in the cap began to feel uneasy.

The tram jolted off and crawled on up the narrow old Moscow street, where three-litre jars, wrapped round with muslin and containing mushrooms like shaggy jellyfish, stood on the window-sills of the wooden houses, next to agave plants with knobbly, antler-like stems. The tram had lived out its days together with these houses, and a kind of sad mutual understanding seemed to exist between them. The orange car went on following the tram and the stare from it continued. The girl in the cap lowered her eyes and with difficulty extracted a copy of *Foreign Literature* magazine from a polythene bag which was crushed against the side. On the bag was a picture of Misha the bear, the hero of the recently finished Olympic Games. She was scarcely able to open the magazine because there was virtually no room between her face and the window. The letters jumped in front of her eyes, forming themselves higgledy-piggledy into phrases totally removed from the puffing fat man with the mirror, from the bottle poking her in the hip, from the two blue balloons inside the seemingly empty truck, and indeed from herself:

*'Yes, I intend to sell my body. And I'm announcing this for all to hear!' said Mary Jane Hackett, on arriving from Kentucky State. 'There's no demand for talent now, so why not simply present them with my body, young and mouthwatering.'*

Looking over her *Foreign Literature* magazine and out of the window, the girl again caught sight of the same relentless eyes, separate from the face. But suddenly, for a second, the windscreen wipers were turned on, little jets of water washed the dust off the windscreen, and the eyes acquired a face. The face was male, strong, almost young, except for harsh wrinkles on a sunburned brow. The head was shaven bare, making him look like a soldier with a year or two behind him or someone just released from prison. The shaven man didn't smile or make eyes at her – he just stared. The girl began to feel as if she wasn't herself: perhaps I'm imagining that he's following me? He's driving behind the tram and that's all there is to it . . . watching the tram, not me at all, not even my cap, thought the girl, and again she took cover behind her copy of *Foreign Literature*. But maybe I secretly want to be followed? And that's why I wear the cap, she thought, jeering at herself, perhaps I'm also a Mary Jane, only still in my infancy. The letters began to jump once more before her eyes, in time to the tram moving along the pre-revolutionary cobbles:

9

*'Tut tut, Mary Jane,' said a tall young man.*

*'And when, I wonder, did you last kiss a girl?' she demanded.*

*'In '28, in honour of Herbert Hoover being elected president,' he replied without a moment's thought.*

*Everyone in the drawing room burst out laughing good-naturedly.*

And it seemed to the girl as if everyone had burst out laughing at her too but that the laughter was not at all good-natured – the fat man with the mirror, making the red tassels dance on his Ukrainian embroidered shirt, the skinny old drunk in his greasy hat, and the once invisible being behind the wheel of the orange car. The girl counted the stops to herself: One, two, three. The next one's mine. She squeezed her *Foreign Literature* magazine into her bag, knocking the peak of her cap against the edge of the mirror, and, forcing her way to the doors, glanced unwillingly in the direction of the window, through the mass of faces and shoulders. Something orange glimmered implacably in the chinks of light. She jumped down from the tram platform, tugging at her polythene bag – the Olympic bear's head had got stuck in the doors as they banged shut. Without looking in the direction of the car she thought miserably: I just hope he doesn't try to chat me up. That's all I need. But when the tram moved on and the girl tried to cross the street, the car's orange side materialized in front of her, and a strong arm flung the door open.

'In you get.'

A removal van hooted indignantly from behind.

'In you get,' ordered the shaven man. 'I can't stop here. I'll explain it all to you in a minute.'

And without knowing why, the girl got in and the car moved off, following the tram as before, accom-

10

panied by the persistent presence of the removal van in the rear mirror.

'What will you explain to me?' asked the girl, not looking at the driver and furiously angry with herself because for some unknown reason she now found herself in this orange car. There was a strange vegetable kind of smell inside it.

'I was following you,' the shaven man answered. 'I was frightened by your face.'

'But I was by yours,' said the girl, flinching.

'You were thinking that life has no meaning,' he continued without listening to her. 'I could see that from your face. But if someone even thinks that life has no meaning, it at once stops being meaningless in the process.'

'Do you trot out that old cliché every time you drive behind trams and eye the women? I hope you don't turn your nose up at buses and trolley buses. I dare say it's a bit more complicated in the metro – you can't drive underground in a Zhiguli, can you now?' asked the girl, but inside she shrank. For I really was thinking how meaningless life is, especially when I saw the bulging eyes of that fat man holding the mirror . . . and then, that bottle in my side. Come to think of it, who doesn't think how meaningless life is when they're being poked from all sides? What kind of a mind-reading philosopher does that make him? It's probably an old trick of a wolf-on-wheels. He puts on an act of sympathizing with women's sufferings written all over their 'fine, tortured faces', a little dealer driving around making out he's the tram passenger's guardian angel. *The French baron kissed the girl of low rank, raising her to his own level* . . . I wonder why it smells like a vegetable patch in here?

'Don't be like that,' said the shaven-headed man

11

without anger. 'All the same, you don't believe what you've just been saying and thinking or you wouldn't have got into my car.'

'But why did I have to get into it?'

'You didn't have to. But you got in, which means you wanted to.'

'I didn't want to at all. That stupid removal van hooting made me lose my head. Stop the car. Where are you taking me?'

'I'm following your tram.'

'I'd already got out of it. I'd got to where I was going.'

'You haven't got anywhere yet. You're still there in the tram. You see, that's your face pressed up against the window. You are thinking how meaningless life is. Then you feel someone staring at you. You still haven't realized who it is. You look round. There's a fat man with a mirror and an old drunk in what used to be a hat. No, it's not them. Then you look up and see me. Not my face but something hazy, because the windscreen is covered in dust. Perhaps you only saw my eyes. They frighten you. You take refuge behind your copy of *Foreign Literature*, but feel me staring at you through the pages. I feel that you need me and so I follow your tram.'

'I don't need anyone.'

'Then you are unhappy. But that is not true, you are simply confused and don't know what to do.'

'Listen, why are you trying to get inside me like this? Stop the car.'

'I'll stop the car when the tram you're still in stops. Now I am turning on the windscreen wipers, and they're washing the dust off the windscreen. Now you can see my face. You are frightened by my shaved head and again protect yourself from me with your

12

*Foreign Literature*, only your cap sticks out above the cover. The tram stops and so do I. You get out of the tram and . . . Stop it! You mustn't open the door from the inside. You haven't opened it from the outside yet. That was the removal van hooting. Now I am telling you, "In you get." Now you've got in, and you still can't understand why you did.'

The girl had made an attempt to open the car door, but his hand had powerfully intercepted her own. Despite the tough movement the hand itself was soft and smooth. The girl was struck by the fact that the hand did not seem strange to her. Nor did his voice seem unfamiliar.

'Don't go away.'

The tram moved off, scattering its passengers' buttons in its wake.

The removal van did not hoot this time, but let out a wail, and the car moved off once more along the tram lines. A rut in the cobbles made it jolt. The girl heard a strange clinking behind her and turned round involuntarily. All the space inside the car was taken up. There were three boxes of bottles clinking, one of champagne, a second of vodka and a third of mineral water. Two enamel buckets, one full of tomatoes and the other of cucumbers, were rocking slightly. Apples and pears were rolling out of a basket and on to the snouts of three sucking-pigs, pale in anticipation of the spit. These were on piles of salad stuff – parsley, dill, tsitsmati, mint, coriander and radishes. That was why the car smelt so like a vegetable patch.

'What's all that?' the girl burst out.

'That is what you and I will now eat and drink,' the driver replied without a smile.

'Listen, don't think I'm going to be a part of some psychological experiment of yours,' said the girl, flying

13

into a rage. 'For the last time, stop the car!'

The driver suddenly turned sharply and braked. The car's right wheels mounted the pavement, causing a musical ringing to travel through the bottles. The removal van rumbled rapidly past, a hairy tattooed fist threatening furiously from it.

The shaven-headed man turned off the ignition, settled back and closed his eyes. The blue balloons, gleaming from within, disappeared under dead eyelids. His face suddenly lost the strength of its features and became lifeless, as if about to collapse. Only the wrinkles on his brow retained their sharpness. There were exactly three of them.

'What is it, can't you hear me?' said the girl almost shouting, unable to restrain her voice.

'I can hear you,' he answered. 'You've got out of the tram, but you still haven't got into my car.'

He's mad, thought the girl. Or maybe he's just ill and he's delirious? Or got DTs? And suddenly, to her horror, she felt herself unable to open the car door – her hand wouldn't move. The feverish thought crossed her mind that he might be a hypnotist.

Why am I sitting here with him, like a fool; why don't I get out of the car? No, he's not trying to hypnotize me . . . and he doesn't look as if he's out to get me. And all at once an unanticipated burst of maternal instinct rose in her, making her guess that he was desperately tired and that all he wanted to do was sleep. Maybe he was asleep already? As he lay back helplessly against the seat there was something in him of the little boy, an absolutely exhausted little boy.

'What's the matter?' she asked, touching his arm gently as if trying to convince herself that he was still alive. 'Are you asleep?'

14

'No, I'm not,' he replied, without opening his eyes. 'But I'm dying to sleep. I haven't slept for three days now.'

'Well, sleep for a while then. If you want I'll sit next to you while you do,' she said, much to her own surprise. She was startled that she hadn't got out and indeed couldn't do so.

'I do want to . . . but as it is I can't. I'll just rest a little. Is that all right?'

She didn't even bother answering that it was, just asked:

'But why haven't you slept for three days?'

'I was trying to establish myself, trying to become a genius,' he said, moving his lips slightly, in an attempt at a smile.

'And did it work?' she asked, attempting a smile which didn't come off either.

'It seems to have done . . . ' He opened his eyes and she saw the red veins that go with lack of sleep around the blue balloons. 'To hell with my genius. But you know it's absolutely vital that I don't die just now. I must be careful with myself, treat myself like a precious jewel. I mustn't fly because aeroplanes crash. I shouldn't drive because some drunken idiot might run into me. It might even be better for me not to go outdoors at all – suppose a brick falls on me. I ought to lock myself away behind the four walls of my laboratory and chain myself up for safety's sake. I think I've made a great discovery. You know it's possible I'm the most needed man in the world today.'

'Many people think that to themselves,' said the girl. 'For some reason I can't stand the face of one particular television announcer. He is absolutely convinced that he is the most essential man in the world. Whereas he's simply a greasy parrot in a jacket and tie.'

'You're not very kind in your observations,' said the man. 'Back in the tram window I noticed that for all the confusion with which you view life you have hard grey eyes. That will save you. Or kill you. Sometimes people become malicious through confusion. I think you even wear the cap out of malice. You wear it for the same reason that I shave my head. I shaved it today. Out of spite. Against whom I don't know exactly, but out of spite. For all that, what sort of person is needed most of all today? In all countries, by everybody, at this very moment?'

The girl sank into thought.

'Someone who could give people a common faith in something,' she stammered earnestly.

'Rubbish!' exclaimed the man with cheerful conviction, coming back to life before her eyes. 'There could never be a common faith for everyone! How could some thug have the same faith in something as an honest man? The whole of Christianity got stuck at that point, and Christianity wasn't the only one. A common faith in something – that's too wishy-washy and insubstantial. One can only combat concrete evil with something concrete. Just think, what specific evil threatens all of us right now?'

'War,' said the girl. 'You haven't invented something to stop the bomb, have you?'

He grew sad and for a moment his blue balloons lost their inner glow.

'No, I haven't, more's the pity,' he said quietly, and again withdrew into himself and closed his eyes. 'But I have created Ardabiola.'

'What?' said the girl, not understanding.

16

'Ar – da – bio – la,' he said, patiently pronouncing it syllable by syllable, without opening his eyes. 'I've never been known for my modesty. My surname is Ardabiev. But I'm not the only one to have that name. It belonged to my father, my grandfather and his father before him. According to family tradition it comes from the words "*Ardu biom* – we fight the Golden Horde".'

'But what is this Ardabiola of yours?'

'It's a plant. Do you want to have a look at it?' He opened his blue eyes, now sparkling again, and without waiting for her to agree, extracted from the pile of salad stuff a perfectly ordinary-looking plant with several small green fruit on it.

'They look like feihoi fruit, don't they?'

'I've never seen one,' admitted the girl. 'That's a Japanese fruit isn't it?'

'Why Japanese? It grows here too, on the shores of the Black Sea,' said Ardabiev huffily.

'I've never been to the sea.'

'You will. The sea won't elude you. But this plant has nothing in common with feihoi. It is the offspring of an insect and another plant.'

He's mad, the girl thought, her misgivings confirmed, and again she wanted to get out of the car, and again she could not. What if he really was a genius?

At this point a lorry sounded the war-cry, not this time from behind but from the right-hand side. It was trying to get through the gates blocked by the orange car. On the gates were the words *Richard Sorge Clothing Factory*.

With a deep sigh Ardabiev drove the car back on to the tram lines.

'Do you know this area?' asked the girl.

A look of embarrassment appeared in his eyes, and

her fear dissolved immediately in their boyish blueness.

'No,' he admitted honestly, 'I was simply following your tram and haven't a clue where we are now.'

'Take the next turning to the right. That's it. Now on a bit, right up to the sign,' ordered the girl. 'Don't worry, there are no police around here. Here we are. We won't be bothered by any removal vans or factory lorries here. Tell me about your Ardabiola . . . '

'It's a canal,' said Ardabiev, delighted by the surprise, and he stopped the car on the bank by the water. There was hardly anyone by the canal, just a little old fisherman with a despairing fishing-rod and an elderly couple sitting on the grass and dipping hard-boiled eggs into an open matchbox of salt. Nearby was their Zaporozhets car, still wet from being washed.

Ardabiev got out of the car and stretched himself, his bones cracking. He turned his face to the sun and again closed his eyes. The girl also got out, but pulled the peak of her cap down a little, for she was loth to let the sun on her face.

'Would you like to eat perhaps?' she asked. 'Have you had breakfast today?'

'I don't think I have,' said Ardabiev uncertainly, only half hearing her and enjoying the sun as it ran over his face.

The girl seized the initiative. 'You've got some lovely tomatoes and cucumbers in the car. Have you got any salt?'

'No,' answered Ardabiev, screwing his eyes up happily.

'Help yourself from the car and get yourself started. I'll just go and get some.'

The girl went up to the elderly couple and came

18

back with a pinch of salt in the palm of her hand. Ardabiev was already sitting on the sand with two cucumbers and two tomatoes on a newspaper. Next to them stood a bottle of champagne.

'That's from tomorrow's birthday spread, is it?' asked the girl, emptying the salt out on to the newspaper.

'Wrong,' said Ardabiev, shaking his shaved head. 'Tomorrow I'm going to "celebrate" getting my higher degree. I've been rushing about like a madman since first thing and I feel completely drained. Do you think it's so easy to lay your hands on three sucking-pigs?'

'No, I don't,' said the girl, smiling naturally for the first time. 'Incidentally, won't they go off?'

'Damn them,' said Ardabiev, dismissing the sucking-pigs with a flick of the wrist. 'It's a pity we can't tuck into them right away. We could give one to that fisherman over there, another to that couple by the Zaporozhets and eat the third ourselves. We could set the champagne and the vodka out in a row on the canal side. Now that'd be the way to celebrate getting a thesis accepted!'

'But what's it on? Is it about Ardabiola?' asked the girl, carefully leading him back to his elusive subject.

'If only it was . . . my thesis isn't worth a thing when compared with Ardabiola.' And he dug his strong, even teeth into a scarlet tomato, forgetting even to put salt on it.

Ardabiev really was both terribly tired and terribly hungry. The girl had guessed right on both scores. Tomato seeds and juice spattered on his brand new dark blue jeans, but he didn't even wipe them off. He pulled the little silver cap off a bottle of champagne and untwisted the wire, and the plastic cork whizzed

19

out into the air with a fountain of foam.

'Half left, I think,' said Ardabiev, looking at the dark green bottle against the light. 'I haven't got any glasses.'

The girl took a sip and put the bottle down out of his reach.

'You shouldn't drink. You haven't slept and you're driving. And I can't drive.'

'You talk to me the way my wife does,' said Ardabiev, grinning. 'I follow a strange girl in a tram for an entire hour and out comes my own wife.'

The girl didn't like this.

'Ardabiola,' she said, 'Tell me about Ardabiola.'

'If you give me the champagne,' said Ardabiev, screwing up his eyes again and lying down on the sand.

'You said that Ardabiola was the offspring of an insect and a plant? Surely that's impossible?'

'The champagne,' pleaded Ardabiev in a low voice.

'Do you need it?'

'It's indispensable.'

'At first I thought you were on the prowl. Then I thought you were mad. But it never occurred to me you were an alcoholic.'

'Word of honour, I'm not an alcoholic. I'm not all that keen on drink even. But right now I absolutely must have a mouthful of champagne.'

'It's warm and nasty.'

'It's got bubbles in it, so it's perfectly all right. I curse you with all the trams and removal vans and all the lorries from all the clothing factories. One mouthful! Or I'll fall asleep for ever and you'll never find out about Ardabiola.'

The girl lifted the bottle to him and he felt it touch his lips. The champagne really was warm and nasty, but there were bubbles in it.

'No, I'm not going to invite the Mishechkins!' he shouted, hitting the grass with his fist. 'They're not coming! They don't deserve any bubbles!'

The girl was patient.

'You've had your drink. Now, Ardabiola . . . '

He crossed his hands behind his head and, with his eyes closed as before, began to talk in a hoarse whisper, as if someone might be able to hear them.

'You think it's absurd that one can cross an insect with a plant? Yet another example of the ignorance of mankind. But there are one or two of us, geneticists, who do know how to do this. What is an insect made up of? Cells. And what is a plant made up of? Cells. Inside each cell is a chromosome, and inside each chromosome are genes. We have found out how to extract the genes from a chromosome. And if one can extract them one can put them together again, in the most varied of combinations. The only thing one has to do is irradiate the genes in the process, so that they don't reject one another. It's something like welding two different metals into one – genetic engineering. Do you follow?'

'Not everything,' answered the girl. 'Won't nature retaliate?'

'She will if we go against her. But if we help her along then we are merely being nature ourselves.'

The girl brushed an ant off Ardabiev's shaven head, so simply that it seemed as if she had stroked his head many times before. She only noticed this gesture of hers after it was done.

'But why did you have to combine an insect and a plant?'

'Have you heard of the tse-tse fly?' he asked, groping blindly for the unfinished bottle on the sand.

21

'Yes, I have. Its bite can cause sleeping sickness,' answered the girl, stealthily moving the bottle away from his hand.

'That's not all it causes. It was discovered that a particular form of cancer, Burkitt's lymphoma, exists in exactly those parts of Africa where the tse-tse fly is found. Don't hide the bottle from me! Just one more mouthful of bubbles. I deserve them, I'm not Mishechkin! Thank you for your compassion. Well, anyway, one day a scientist discovered a kind of tse-tse fly strain on which he could grow an anti-cancer substrate.'

'Strain? Substrate?' The girl bit a blade of grass with a brown feathery top to it.

'A strain, that's a species, I suppose. A substrate, well, let's say a substance – the basis of a substance. But this strain and substrate were lost. The scientist died. It's a sad story, though I don't think that substrate was a panacea for all kinds of cancer. Cancer is many different tragedies of the organism, which we call by one name only because we don't know any better. Maybe we should open another bottle of champagne?'

'No,' said the girl firmly. 'We're not having a second bottle. Don't lose your thread.

Ardabiev submitted. 'I'm not. The bubbles are all I'm losing. I've still got the thread.

'Just what is cancer? An infection? The result of nerve cells disintegrating? No one knows exactly. Apparently certain definite carcinogens have been found – nicotine for example – but smokers aren't the only ones to get lung cancer. So with your permission I shall now smoke, and not feel as if I'm sentencing myself to death. And what if there are psychological carcinogens? Couldn't the thoughts we repress inside us be carcinogens, for instance? The ancients called cancer the disease of the bile, the disease that goes with a gloomy sense of life. Couldn't pessimism be a carcinogen?'

'I used to know someone who was optimistic to the point of dottiness,' said the girl, shaking her head. 'But he died of cancer.'

'No one knows what he was like when he was alone. Often people who strain every nerve, making out they are optimists, are actually riddled with secret germs. Cancer is obviously an infection, but it is easier for an infection to make its way into a body with weak psychological defences. What if fatigue is also a carcinogen? Every infection is a poison, and nature is so extraordinary that she has an antidote for every poison. Sometimes, however, this antidote is scattered about in a variety of places. You just have to find it, work out what goes with what and put it together. Nature solves the problems she sets herself through our brains. Even such criminal brains as mine. Go on, admit you thought I was a criminal.'

'Don't ramble,' said the girl severely. 'Stick to the point. Keep to Ardabiola.'

'I am,' said Ardabiev obediently. 'Ardabiola was not invented by Ardabiev. It was created by nature, but spread among different genes. Ardabiev had the hunch that this was so. There was fedyunnik first of all. Ah! You don't know what it is? But then do you know the name of the piece of grass you're chewing, with the brown feathery top to it? You don't! And neither do I. But it does have a name, and it may be that one of nature's unsolved powers is entering you right now, along with its sap. You might be acquiring immunity against lateral sclerosis of the spinal cord, say. Animals have subtler instincts than we do, and

23

can sense which grass they need to chew during a particular illness. But even people sense something. All our folk medicine derives from those instincts that haven't been killed off.'

'Won't you burn in the sun? Your nose has already started to,' warned the girl. 'Or is this your favourite position for lecturing – lying down with your eyes closed? Well then, fedyunnik?'

'I come from Siberia. Fedyunnik is a kind of bushy plant like a bog whortleberry, but with brownish, nasty-tasting berries. It is an old custom in our area to eat them if you have a cancerous tumour. Or they can be dried and drunk as an infusion. But what's more, people eat them when they are unhappy in love. Fedyunnik doesn't just work against tumours, it's also an anti-depressant. There's even a little tune about it. May I sing it to you?'

And without opening his eyes or getting up from the grass, he quietly began to sing:

'Off went my dearest,
Though I clung to his shoe,
So I ran to the forest:
"Oh fedyunnik, help me do!"
Alone, I lost my reason,
Alone, I sat a-grieving,
Two berries I decided on,
A third needed no bidding!
While a fourth little berry
Shook my spirits loose,
And it made me so merry,
I no longer craved a noose . . .

It's nice, isn't it? Even when I sing it.'

'Yes,' said the girl. 'But what do you do when your head's already in a noose and the berry is only between your teeth?'

24

'First, swallow the berry,' answered Ardabiev, trying to sound sure of himself, but hesitating. 'As long as it's not a poisonous one, of course.'

'You don't know until you've swallowed it,' said the girl frowning, and suddenly she bit her lip as if she was in pain. She went slightly pale.

But Ardabiev did not see this. His eyes were closed, tortured by lack of sleep, his face thrown back to face the sun. It had been a long time since he had lain in the sun with his eyes closed, with warm sand under his head – able to pick up handfuls of it with an outstretched hand and to unclasp his fingers slowly, feeling time swish through them.

'A holiday . . . I must go on holiday somewhere,' he muttered inaudibly to himself. 'Just to sleep or lie like this in the sun. Not to think. Lucky Mishechkin! How proudly he once announced, "I turn my consciousness right off when I'm on holiday." The trouble is he forgets to switch it back on when he gets back. But maybe he's also lucky in that. I've got some kind of curse on me. I don't know how to switch myself off. I like this girl. God knows why, but I do, though not to make a pass at. I'm thinking about myself again, like a machine, dragging her into my thoughts. While she probably doesn't know how to get away from her own. Something has happened to her, is happening to her. She has already swallowed some kind of poisonous berry. But suppose she's swallowed more than one? I could give her some of my Ardabiola. But maybe she needs something completely different. Why am I thinking about this girl instead of stroking her hand?'

'Is your father alive?' he asked.

'I think so,' answered the girl reluctantly.

'What do you mean, you think so?'

25

'I've never set eyes on him.'

'I'm sorry,' said Ardabiev, understanding.

Still lying on the bank next to the orange car, Ardabiev suddenly lifted his heavy, wilful eyelids. The shiny blue balloons appeared once more from underneath them and looked at the girl intently. The girl turned her eyes away. Ardabiev sat down on the sand, hugged his knees and avoided looking at her. He felt it would be easier for her that way. He knew she didn't want him to know too much about her.

'Why have you stopped talking?' asked the girl. 'You began telling me about fedyunnik. You even sang.'

Ardabiev did not look at her, as if observing an unspoken contract. But he saw her. Not here, next to him on the dune above the canal but back on the tram platform.

When she had taken cover from him behind her *Foreign Literature*, he had all the same seen her profile in the mirror held by the fat man in the Ukrainian shirt. She had a proud, well-defined chin line rising above a fragile neck, almost transparent in the light and dotted with birthmarks. The girl tried to give everyone, even herself, the impression that no one on earth could hurt her. But her childish protruding lips betrayed a hurt that had already been inflicted.

Ardabiev began to speak, as if continuing to look through the window of the tram:

'You know, I never imagined that my father could fall ill. There just didn't seem to be a single little hole in him for illness to crawl into. At sixty he was driving an engine on the Trans-Siberian railway, hunting and fishing, outdrinking everybody but never falling into a ditch. Then suddenly he began to get pains in his chest. When they told him the diagnosis – secondary

26

tumours in the lungs – he ran away from the hospital, took his gun and rucksack and went into the taiga to die. But six weeks later he returned, alive and well. The secondaries had disappeared. He had been saved by fedyunnik. The doctors called it a miracle, but warned him it might turn out to be a temporary one.'

The childish lips in the fat man's mirror tightened so that sharp wrinkles formed in their corners. She was still so young that she had only to smile for those wrinkles to disappear. But one day, treacherously, they wouldn't go away, even if she roared with laughter. Smiling would make them deeper still.

'I was sent to Africa at the time. The trip didn't have anything to do with cancer, but I was thinking about my father. I remembered that old, perhaps lost, idea of an anti-cancer substrate. Do you remember what a substrate is?'

There on the tram platform the childish lips with their nascent wrinkles did not relax. But a voice that came from within, like a ventriloquist's, answered:

'Yes, I do . . .'

'I found the lost tse-tse fly strain. When I got back I extracted a gene from the tse-tse fly chromosome and combined it with a fedyunnik gene. I cultivated Ardabiola – imagine, in my own flat. In an ordinary wooden box with ordinary soil. The same bush, the same leaves, but instead of the brown berries, green fruit appeared, like feihoi, only smaller.'

The tram jolted, making the mirror swing in the hands of the fat man and the girl's face fell from it. The mirror began to sway like a patchwork blanket sewn together of other incidental faces.

'I got hold of a rat which had been injected with methyl nitrosourea, a very powerful carcinogen. This induced a tumour. To my wife's horror I kept the rat

27

in the birdcage, letting free the canary – much to its delight. For some reason, I called the rat Alla. I kept her half-starved and began to slip Ardabiola in with her food. At first Alla only sniffed the fruit and refused to eat. Then I began to talk to her. I explained how important it was both for her and for human beings. My wife decided that I had finally gone off my head and gave me an ultimatum: "It's me or the rat." I chose the rat. Alla obeyed me and began to eat Ardabiola. Generally she proved herself to be a clever little thing. After a week I noticed that a spark of life had appeared in her dull, sad little eyes. Her coat began to shine and the coordination she had partly lost returned. She began to run from one corner of her cage to another. One morning a month later I saw that three of the birdcage wires had been gnawed through and Alla had disappeared. I called her name, and she crawled out from underneath the kitchen cupboard at my bidding. I felt I was betraying her. I took her in my hands and begged her to forgive me for the fact that I had to kill her. I even began to weep. When they opened Alla up it turned out that the tumour had vanished. I shared my discovery with only one man, my colleague Mishechkin. He made a laughing stock of me and called it all "scientific mysticism".'

'Excuse me, you don't need this bottle?' asked a gentle voice. A tiny old woman with beady eyes, holding a champagne bottle in one hand and a clanking sack in the other, had sprung up in front of Ardabiev and the girl.

'I picked this bottle up near the fisherman, thinking it was his. But he goes and nods at you, saying as how it's yours. I don't have much use for them dark green ones, I like bottles you can see through. So you don't need this one, do you?'

'No,' said Ardabiev, beginning to laugh and turning to the girl: 'You see, we should have drunk the second bottle, in honour of this old lady . . . '

'I can easily wait,' said the old woman readily. 'Where have I got to hurry off to?'

'The day after tomorrow,' promised Ardabiev, 'I'll bring a whole lot of empty bottles to this very spot.' Gratefully but not without her doubts the old woman nodded and began hobbling on, prodding the bushes with her stick.

Still not wanting to look Ardabiev in the eyes the girl turned her face to the canal. He saw that some of her straight fair hair was gathered up at the back of her head, under her cap, while some flowed freely down, falling to her shoulders. The hairline at the back of her head was just below the rim of the cap, and another dark birthmark stood out right on this line. There was no fat man with a mirror nearby, and Ardabiev could not see the girl's face. But you can make someone out from their back as well as from their face. Her back was exhausted. It listened but thought of something of its own, about which it did not want to think.

'Go on,' said the girl insistently. 'Don't stop talking.'

'The pains in my father's chest began again. He flew to Moscow. For the first time I saw him morbid and depressed. I got him into the Kashirskaya hospital. They pumped out the fluid in his chest, began chemotherapy and radiation treatment but said there was no hope; secondary piled upon secondary. I took my father home and told him about the tse-tse fly, about fedyunnik and about Alla. I told him it was a risk. He agreed to try. I had only twelve Ardabiola

29

fruit left. I gave them to my father in segments and made an infusion of the leaves. The pains stopped immediately. His hair stopped falling out and began to grow again. After a month they did all the tests again. The doctors could not believe their eyes, the tumour had remitted.'

'Had what?' the girl asked.

'Had disappeared. My father went home and is now back driving his engine. But I held my tongue. I didn't have a single fruit left. I resolved to be patient and nurtured my Ardabiola with all the fertilizers on earth. You had the second crop of Ardabiola in your hands. Early this morning, even before going to look for those wretched sucking-pigs, I went to the Institute of Organic Chemistry for them to do a precise analysis of Ardabiola. If there is a similar chemical substance then mankind has an extremely powerful weapon against cancer in its hands. However, by one of life's mean tricks the laboratory was shut today. They've all gone digging potatoes. But what does that matter? Today or tomorrow, the main thing is that Ardabiola exists!'

Ardabiev leapt up from the sand and suddenly shouted out to all the canalside, triumphantly waving his arms:

'Ar – da – bio – la!'

The elderly couple hurriedly poured their eggshells into a folded scrap of paper torn from *Ogonyok* magazine and headed timidly for their now dry Zaporozhets.

But the fisherman with his despondent fishing-rod did not even seem to hear.

Suddenly Ardabiev saw that the girl in the cap had begun to reel rather strangely to one side. Her face had grown pale.

'What's the matter?' said Ardabiev, rushing towards her. 'Have I worn you out with all my talk of cancer or something?'

'N-no,' said the girl, shaking her head. 'I'm ill . . . it's my fault. I was going to the hospital. Could you take me back there?'

The distraught Ardabiev caught her under the arms and sat her in the car. The hospital was next to the tram stop where the girl had got off two hours earlier.

'You don't have to come in with me,' said the girl, gritting her teeth against the pain.

Refusing to listen, Ardabiev took her to the reception area.

'Look, she's crammed her cap on all right,' spluttered a woman in the corridor behind the girl. 'Even if she hasn't actually been able to stand on her feet since morning. Well that's young people for you!'

'Go,' said the girl to Ardabiev, swaying as she pulled the door handle towards her.

'That cap! Take it off at once, you cheeky girl!' came a hissing voice behind her.

Ardabiev stayed in the corridor, sitting down on a squeaky chair right in the middle of all the clamour. It stopped.

Spluttering like that's a dreadful habit, especially in hospital, thought Ardabiev. But I can't talk – holding forth about saving mankind and not even noticing that the person I was with was ill. No, I noticed it right back there in the tram window and that's why I followed the tram. But then I forgot and went off into a monologue.

Half an hour later Ardabiev was on the point of knocking on the cubicle door when it flew open and a bed on castors was wheeled out. Only the girl's face protruded from beneath the sheet, hardly differing

31

from it in colour. The girl's eyelids were closed but quivered slightly. The bed was pushed along a corridor which seemed endless to Ardabiev. A hand fell on his shoulder. In front of him stood a young doctor with an indifferent and unfriendly face.

'Did you bring her in?'

'Yes,' answered Ardabiev dejectedly.

'Come into my office,' said the doctor.

Ardabiev went in and the doctor opened the admissions book without inviting him to sit down.

'What's the matter with her?' said Ardabiev.

'Heavy internal bleeding,' said the doctor. 'Who carried out the abortion?'

'I don't know,' muttered Ardabiev.

'It was done by a quack. You can do someone lasting harm that way,' said the doctor, hostile by now. 'She had almost lost consciousness, and I wasn't able to admit her formally. Her surname?'

'I don't know,' said Ardabiev, bowing his head.

'Well, what about her first name? Where does she live? Or work? Or study?'

'I don't know anything about her,' said Ardabiev, without looking up. 'I simply gave her a lift here.'

The doctor's face remained suspicious and hostile. He closed the book and got up, making it clear that the conversation was at an end.

'It isn't dangerous, is it?' asked Ardabiev, not moving.

'They're giving her a blood transfusion right now. That is all I can tell you,' he said, adding unkindly, 'especially as you say you don't know her.'

Driving out of the hospital courtyard, Ardabiev was forced to brake in front of a tram with the same number on it as before. However, it was not the eyes of a girl in a cap that looked at him, but the troubled inquiring eyes of a thin boy in a Young Pioneer's neckerchief, trying to read and using an elbow to shield his book from a roll of Vietnamese matting.

What if this boy is the person of most use to mankind today, that it's not me at all? thought Ardabiev. Suppose he can give everyone a common faith in something? Or invent something to stop the bomb?

The tram sucked in new passengers and moved off, but the orange car stayed where it was until an exasperated hoot sounded from behind.

Ardabiev looked in the mirror; once again a removal van had nearly gone into his bumper. It could have been a different one, but it looked the same, and its contents were probably similar. As he watched the furious but nevertheless majestic face of the removal van driver, indignantly leaning out of his cab, Ardabiev grinned bitterly: and maybe he's convinced he's the man of most use to mankind today as well.

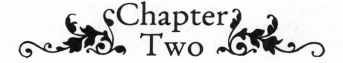

# Chapter Two

The engine driver, Ardabiev senior, was changing in the depot shower room, opening his personal locker, which for forty years had borne his name, with his own personal key. His name had remained untouched on the locker even during the four years he had been at the front. From his work clothes came a particular railway smell, consisting of grease, tarred sleepers, the taiga wind and something else you couldn't put your finger on. Ardabiev had started on the railway as a greaser, heaving the oil-can, known as 'the goose' because of its outstretched neck, along the axle-boxes. Then he became a stoker on the old steam engines, and his overalls had smelt of coal. The tiniest splinters of it used to get into his nostrils, ears, hair and behind his collar. The young stoker used to change after work into crinkly box-calf boots, casual trousers with concertina pleats and a snow-white shirt with a round collar and cufflinks, and put on the velveteen waistcoat and pocket watch chain he had got from his father. Then he would go out dancing with other depot lads just like him, and when they spat with their particular flair on the creaking wooden pavement, their spittle would still be black. Then they brought in the electric engines, the stoker's job disappeared and the job of driver became a cleaner one, though even before it had been considered the aristocrat among railway jobs. It was still Ardabiev's habit to go and steam himself, although ten layers of dirt no longer came off him as they used to. He took the bundle of birch twigs he had prepared beforehand from his locker and headed first of all into the steam room, where several naked figures stood out against the haze.

'Andrei Ivanovich, hello!' said the owner of a comfortable round tummy, rocking on two legs with large calf muscles and red hairs.

Ardabiev recognized Pestrukhin, the head of the personnel department, whose habitual execessive attentiveness and sugary sweetness did not particularly endear him to Ardabiev.

'Give me your bunch of birch twigs, Andrei Ivanovich,' said Pestrukhin, beginning to bustle about him. 'I'll give you such a going over now, you'll remember the name of Pestrukhin for ever. Don't you worry, I'll scald the birch twigs myself. I know my stuff. Just lie down here, on the second ledge. I've already splashed it with boiling water. Relax, Andrei Ivanovich, relax. Is there enough steam for you? If not, maybe I should pour on some more water?'

'What is that stench?' said Ardabiev, sniffing the air. 'It smells like a chemist's in here.'

'What indeed is that stench, if you'll excuse the expression, Andrei Ivanovich,' said Pestrukhin, slightly offended, 'but the little bit of menthol I sprinkled in the water scoop. In a word, an inhalation for us!'

And the bunch of birch twigs set off on its travels across Ardabiev's back. Pestrukhin roamed about him deftly, at times flicking the leaves over his body, at times tickling his heels, and then he'd scratch right across him, and there would be no holding back a moan.

'Well, your body, Andrei Ivanovich, I'll tell you straight, it's superb! No one would take you for sixty. Not an ounce of fat, it's all muscle. At forty-six I'm

36

already having to attack my own paunch with the birch twigs. But you know the kind of work I do, sitting down busying myself with papers all day, it's not like yours,' said Pestrukhin, his oily eyes staring into Ardabiev's from under his felt head shield. This reminder of his age, though also flattering, set Ardabiev on guard. Or perhaps it was precisely because it was flattering that he felt wary?

'But I thought you were ill with something, weren't you, Andrei Ivanovich? Didn't you even fly to Moscow? You'd never guess now from the shape you're in. What were you ill with?'

'Nothing,' said Ardabiev, cutting him short. 'I haven't been off sick once in my life yet. I went to Moscow to visit my son.'

'I've never been off sick either, Andrei Ivanovich, but as for being ill, I've been that all right. See that red square on my backside, excuse the expression, that's the mark from the pepper plaster I had when I was plagued with neuritis. They were smoking away at a meeting, and I upped and opened the window opposite my chair right then and there. That's how I caught it. So when I was asking you about your illness just now, it wasn't to trip you up,' chirped Pestrukhin, sensing that Ardabiev was suspicious. 'But now you beat me with the twigs, Andrei Ivanovich. Go on, flog the old bureaucrat. That's it. That's the way. What a nice exchange of courtesies.'

Wrapped in a towel in the changing room, Pestrukhin plunged his hand smartly into his briefcase and drew out a bottle of beer:

'It's Mongolian, off the Ulan-Bator train. There's only one bottle I'm afraid. I didn't expect to meet . . .'

He opened the bottle nimbly on the edge of the

bench and handed it to Ardabiev.

'You first, Andrei Ivanovich. You're the senior . . . '

Ardabiev took a sip, silently noting this last remark. They're creeping up on me, cunningly creeping up on me, he thought, suddenly tired and disgusted.

Pestrukhin drained his half and wheezed:

'They're all right, our Mongolian brothers!' Fastening his watch strap and eyeing the time, he began to hurry:

'Goodness, it's half six already. My better half will probably have got fed up with waiting for me by now.'

He went out, thriftily putting the empty bottle back in his briefcase. One of the depot metal-workers, once a well-covered man, who had a mouse tattooed on one skinny buttock and a cat on the other, sighed with relief:

'Pestrukhin doesn't wash the soap off even when he showers. He's a slippery fish all right, not a man at all . . . '

'He was making hints about my age, Ivan,' said Ardabiev. 'It's time I retired, of my own accord, before they start asking me to. It's time to grow vegetables.'

'Leave off talking about your vegetables,' said the metal-worker, slapping him on his bare back. 'You're a champion engine-driver. You'll be made an instructor. There aren't any champion metal-workers, you know. Listen, let's go drinking today, shall we, eh?'

'I don't know,' said Ardabiev, climbing into a clean shirt. 'I like drinking in a good mood. Vodka doesn't change one's mood, it just enhances it, and I'm in a bad mood.'

'So what's up with you then? Old age? It's not death, you know.'

'It's death for me,' answered Ardabiev. 'I don't feel

38

my age, understand? But I feel as if they're pushing me into it, like into a gas-chamber.'

'Stop going on like this. It's not like you. It's true you're strong now, but all the same you ought to retire while you're going strong, and then you won't be laughed at,' said the metal-worker, tying up the drawstring on his pants.

'Well, why aren't you retiring then? You're the same age as me.'

'I already have,' said the metal-worker, lowering his eyes.

'When?' asked Ardabiev, amazed.

'Yesterday. I took the application to Pestrukhin, and he soaped me all over with gratitude. He began trying to talk me out of it, if only for decency's sake. His eyes are so oily you couldn't even wash them clean with paraffin. And so, Andrei, I'm in these showers for the last time. I won't be coming to steam in here any more. I'll leave my locker key in the keyhole.'

The metal-worker took a penknife from his jacket and neatly started scraping off the words 'I. Vesyolykh' engraved – probably by the very same penknife – on the light blue locker.

Soon I'll be leaving my key and scraping my name off like that, thought Ardabiev.

'But why such a rush about it all?' asked Ardabiev gingerly. 'Has something had a go at the cat or mouse on your behind?'

The metal-worker looked round to make sure there was no one else in the changing room apart from them and said to him:

'You, thank God, have never been ill and aren't ill now. But I'm in a bad way, Andrei. I've got cancer of the liver.'

Ardabiev breathed out:

39

'What are you babbling on about? Who told you? This is one thing our doctors won't talk about. They won't tell you, even if you do have cancer.'

'I sensed it myself. When they did the tests on me at Irkutsk their faces began to darken and I saw the pity in the doctors' eyes. I got up and said to them: "I'm not made of glass, I won't break. I've got cancer, haven't I?" They answered: "Yes, you have." I asked if it was curable. They answered: "We'll do all we can." The doctors were good. They tried. They gave me radiotherapy. It helped a bit. They gave me an extra six months.'

'Did you try fedyunnik?'

'Yes, I did. Obviously it was too late. I had neglected my liver . . . Pestrukhin didn't leave any Mongolian beer, did he? Shame. I've already got the cancer – "It's just the beer that's missing", as Svetlov* said,' and he burst out laughing, though not with his eyes.

'And what now?' asked Ardabiev, feeling as if he were to blame.

His son had forbidden him to talk about Ardabiola until the new crop had grown and a chemical analysis had been carried out on it to confirm its value.

'I'm going to Yesenin† now,' said the metal-worker.

'To which Yesenin?' said Ardabiev, not understanding.

'To *the* Yesenin!'

'He died long ago.'

'He didn't die naturally, he hanged himself,' said the metal-worker. 'I want to do homage at

---

*Mikhail Svetlov, Soviet poet, 1903–1973
†Sergei Yesenin, Russian poet, 1895–1925

his grave in Moscow, and then I'm going to Konstan-
tinovo.'

'You won't help yourself or him by doing that . . .'

'Neither of us have any use for help now. It's too
late. So call in this evening for a drink, eh?'

'You shouldn't be drinking.'

'I can do anything I want now.' And putting down
his penknife, the metal-worker picked up his battered
little case and walked out of the changing room.

I must call in. Oh, Ivan, Ivan, thought Ardabiev.
But didn't I promise my wife we'd go to an Indian
film today? Why has everyone here gone mad about
Indian films?

Ardabiev walked out of the shower room, and for
the first time his little case – exactly the same as Ivan
Vesyolykh's – seemed heavy to him. He walked past
the massive depot, into which the engines were
crawling to recover, hushed and tired after work, past
Lenin – gleaming with still wet silver paint – his arm
thrown up above the station square. Ardabiev went
up the grooved iron steps to the overhead platform
thrown across the Trans-Siberian Railway, and slowed
his pace, looking down at the apparent confusion of
rails, at the semaphores flashing different colours, at
the lights on the points and at the green caterpillar of
the Moscow-Vladivostok express, pausing briefly
alongside the platform. Suddenly he caught sight of
the familiar old shunting engine on which he had
started off as a stoker. Throwing out black smoke and
sparks through its long, old-fashioned funnel as it
always did, the steam engine was pulling empty trucks
along, efficiently building a goods train. It was now
used only for instruction. Youths from the railway
school looked proudly out of its window. The
ingrained spots of coal they wore so happily on their

faces were like signs of their initiation into a special circle of chosen. He thought how the little engine had proved to be tougher than the many people it had outlived, and that it would probably outlive him too. Suddenly he was filled with a desire to get to it and to those youths, that his work clothes might once again smell of coal. By now he could have been teaching them how to stoke the coal in the fire-box and stop sparks flying needlessly out of the funnel.

Ardabiev looked up and saw the dark taiga swaying beyond the last signal-posts of the station, beneath stars which were pale but already stood out against the sky. Mercilessly hacked down, damaged by campfires that hadn't been put out properly, and by idiotic chemical sprays that killed healthy trees along with sick ones, the taiga nevertheless went on struggling for its very existence; it had not succumbed and it retained its beauty and strength no matter what. Just the thought that the taiga still existed made Ardabiev feel easier. He went down the steps of the overhead platform to the other side of Khairiuzovsk, cut in two by the rails.

Here there were more of the old Siberian five-walled houses with their fretted window casings and heavy shutters, bolted fast at night. They were surrounded by mounds of earth, each covered with a green layer of moss. Several of the little wooden houses had subsided, and the windows with their clay pots of bright scarlet geraniums were level with the ground. But each little house had preserved its character, and the featureless breeze-block buildings intruding on the town had a foreign look to them. In these buildings lived the people who had come to build the giant industrial complex, bringing their own way of talking and their nomadic customs to this little town with its native Siberian dialect. The construction people worked very hard, yet it sometimes upset Ardabiev that many of them, even though they hadn't finished building the complex, were already thinking about the next one. The breeze-block buildings with all their conveniences were really just tents for them to camp in, with only cut flowers in the windows, rather than lasting pot plants. Probably through lack of time, many of the builders were not even interested in who lived next door. They did not care who was buried in the cemetery next to the nursery school with its model houses and painted swings. The construction workers' children, born somewhere between two building sites, used to play there. But the history of Siberia lay in the graves of the old Khairiuzovsk cemetery. Here lay Ardabiev's great-grandfather, exiled at some time from Vladimir province for setting fire to his landlord's estate. There lay his grandfather, who had built the Tsarist railroad on the taiga marshes. There lay his father, an engine-driver who had derailed a train during the Civil War by despatching a White officer to the next world with his poker. Ardabiev knew that after his death his place would be at the Khairiuzovsk cemetery too. Work on the complex had gone on for several years and some of the construction workers had died – some from disease, others from industrial accidents – but their cemetery was separate; it had no crosses and more often than not the gravestones were breeze-blocks. It was as if two worlds had come about in Khairiuzovsk, the 'local' one and the 'industrial complex'. The industrial complex children went to a separate school and never chewed the larch resin 'ear-wax' like the locals but only chewing-gum brought from Moscow, Tallin or even America.

Seeing the words 'All Tickets Sold' over the cinema box-office and next to it a crowd of Indian-film worshippers, Ardabiev sighed, thinking of his wife who had probably got herself decked out by now. Suddenly three youths came up to him, dressed like triplets in identical Japanese leather zip-up jackets. The construction workers got these jackets on coupons. So Ardabiev assumed they were industrial complex children. The fact that one of them wasn't an industrial complex child at all, but Pestrukhin's son, didn't enter his head.

'Need to score a ticket?' asked one of the youths, an orthodox cross tumbling over his shirt, visible through the open zip of his Japanese jacket.

Ardabiev did not understand the expression immediately, but then guessed and nodded reluctantly.

'How many?' asked the youth in businesslike fashion.

'Two,' answered Ardabiev awkwardly.

'Three roubles,' said the youth precisely. 'Middle of the tenth row.'

Hating himself, Ardabiev gave him a three-rouble note and began to hurry – there was only half an hour left till the film began.

The front steps of his clean, well-tended house, its railings entwined with pink trumpet flowers, creaked with pleasure as Ardabiev ran up. His wife took his case on the doorstep, as she had for close on forty years, and he said in a deliberately complaining tone:

'Well, mother, you haven't forgotten about the cinema, have you? What's this feast you've laid out?' And he didn't even sit down at the table, laid with orange-peel liqueur, cucumbers and jellied meat.

He knew just from the smell that she hadn't forgotten about the cinema. She was wearing the

'White Lilac' scent which Ardabiev couldn't stand but kept quiet about. Giving her a sidelong glance, he saw that she had been at the hairdresser's that day, where she had had her implacably greying hair dyed and curled. She had slipped her grandmother's silver earrings with their tiny garnets through her earlobes. She had put lipstick on her lips, and had donned a flowery crêpe-de-Chine dress, too bright for her age, and a white plastic belt. On her feet were patent leather but low-heeled shoes. Her stockings however were not sheer but cheap, dark ones, because bumpy varicose veins had started to appear on her legs. She was seven years younger than Ardabiev, but had aged far more than he and was jealous of younger women with more beautiful legs. She was in charge of a chemist's and, when Ardabiev called in on her at work, was secretly glad that the legs of the pretty young sales girls were hidden by the counter and he didn't have a chance to compare them. Ardabiev did not like going to the cinema and therefore this was a rare outing for her. It wasn't so much going to the cinema that she liked, but being seen by everyone to be going to the cinema together with her husband. At the same time it was a torment for her, because there were vast numbers of beautiful women's legs in the street, which Ardabiev could look at and which would make him think how old and unattractive she was. She feared this all the more since their three grown-up children had left and she and Ardabiev lived alone.

'Pestrukhin's been making hints,' said Ardabiev, leading his wife by the arm and nodding soberly at the old women watching people live their lives from behind the moss-covered mounds of earth.

'What about?' asked his wife anxiously.

'What do you think? About my age of course.'

45

She calmed down immediately. His age was the one hope she had that no one would take him away.

'Ivan Vesyolykh has retired of his own accord,' said Ardabiev. 'He's ill. He told me today.'

'What's up with him, then?'

'The same thing.'

'Well, God saved you,' sighed his wife.

'Our son saved me,' corrected Ardabiev severely.

He knew that his wife believed in God, and didn't interfere in this, but didn't associate himself with it either.

'Thus God's power is scattered among different people,' said his wife.

'Why don't you wear a cross if you believe in God?' asked Ardabiev suddenly. 'I came across a lad at the cinema with a cross hanging out on his chest like this . . .'

'That's not believing,' said his wife, shaking her head. 'That's just fashion. A cross is meant to be worn next to your body, not over a shirt or blouse. But you don't even have to wear one on your body. The main thing is that it should be inside you.'

'It'd scratch,' joked Ardabiev morosely, thinking about Ivan Vesyolykh.

While boatloads of Indian women floated by across the screen, wrapped in colourful fabrics and singing doleful but beautiful songs, Ardabiev went on thinking about the depot metal-worker Ivan Vesyolykh, who was leaving the following day to visit Yesenin before he died, and who was probably now sitting and drinking in his own one-man wooden house. And Ardabiev thought: why, instead of dying, couldn't Ivan Vesyolykh find shelter, even if it were inappropriate, on one of these boats; why couldn't he rest his chin on his shabby case, dip a thoughtful hand in the

46

unfamiliar waters of the Ganges, and listen to these Indian songs which he had surely only heard in the cinema? Ardabiev thought about how he too hadn't ever been abroad. The map of the earth is large and human life is short. It is short even without wars and disease, but wars and disease diminish it still further.

Ardabiev cast a sidelong glance at his wife. He could not see her wrinkles in the semi-darkness of the cinema, only her profile, which made her look younger. It was nearly as it had been when they first went to the cinema together, to see the film *If War Breaks Out Tomorrow*. In that, enemy tanks had crossed the Soviet frontier. The screen showed the steppe, out of which a hillock suddenly materialized, together with feather-grass and clumps of earth. It turned out to be a telescopic look-out post. A vigilant pair of binoculars peeped out from it. Then the hillock disappeared and the steppe became level. A Red Army officer climbed down an iron spiral staircase holding the binoculars. He went into an underground hangar, where aeroplanes painted with a red star stood at the ready. At the siren alert the earth moved apart and menacing squadrons flew out towards the enemy.

'Oh how splendid!' she had exclaimed, delightedly clapping her hands. She had been a young girl then, selling the medicines that needed no prescription at the chemist's, with strong shapely legs which were hidden by the counter while she was at work. The war had turned out to be nothing like as short and attractive as it had appeared in the film. In '41, under a terrible, oppressive sky, crowded with German bombers, Ardabiev had gone down on all fours and heaved a shell-shocked Ivan Vesyolykh over the very same feather-grass that they had seen on the pre-war

47

screen. The earth had not opened up, and menacing squadrons had not flown out of it. And now Vesyolykh was going away to die, and maybe would not make it to Yesenin, just as Yesenin probably hadn't made it to someone else.

'Klavdia . . .'

'Do you want to go to Ivan's?' she asked, without turning round. 'Go then.' She was hurt, but understood. 'But mind you don't overdo it,' she whispered after him.

If on his way to Ivan Vesyolykh's Ardabiev had looked carefully at the industrial complex nursery school next to the old Khairiuzovsk cemetery, he would have seen the three triplet-like youths in their identical jackets. They were sitting on three children's swings, the steel ropes creaking slightly. The youths had long since outgrown them and had to draw their legs up to swing. A cheap bottle of wine passed from hand to hand. They took it in turns to swig from it, but the youth with the Orthodox cross, glimmering through the open zip of his jacket, held the bottle between his lips longer than the others, as if he had an unwritten but inalienable right to do so. Under his long, girlish eyelashes were frightening, lifeless eyes. 'I'm bored,' he said, lazily pushing off from the ground with his feet. 'Bored with not drinking and bored with drinking, especially this rubbish. However much you kid yourself, this rough stuff isn't the White Horse your father has in his cabinet, Fantomas. That's an animal you don't see every day in Khairiuzovsk. Why it's a horse you can't forget, if you get what I mean.'

'Yeah, Filosofer,' said a fat youth with white eyebrows like an albino rabbit, obediently jumping off the swing and vanishing into the darkness. The other youth stopped swinging, also ready to jump off and disappear into the night if necessary. He had a Boney M. badge on his jacket and a pinched, freckled nose that pointed up in expectation. His eyes – ginger like the freckles and still quite childish – gleamed with a simultaneous thirst for and fear of instructions. But for the moment there were none.

The youth nicknamed Filosofer went on swinging, really letting himself go now. His face would fall into a strip of light from the nursery school window, then dive into the darkness. But each time it emerged from the night it changed. His eyes became glassy, his features stony. Filosofer was thinking. The swing flew higher and higher, and his face left the light for longer and longer. When it returned, the darkness it had gathered there, up above, remained within his eyes, intense but lifeless. By now he was swinging right up to the level of the cross bar.

'You'll fall, Filosofer!' called the freckled youth in fear.

'Shut up, Speckles!' came a shriek of laughter from above.

Filosofer was swinging higher than the cross bar now. But the cable began to make a grinding noise and the steel loop jumped out of its hook on the beam. The swing crashed to the ground. Filosofer lay still with his face down in the relentless strip of light from the window. Speckles jumped up from his swing and rushed towards him. But Filosofer pushed him away maliciously, crawling out of the strip of light and into the darkness. He sat down on the fence round the children's sand-pit, licking his grazed palm. Then he caught sight of Fantomas, running up out of breath, his white eyebrows shining in the night, and stretched out his hand. A miniature bottle of White Horse whisky appeared in it. Filosofer first splashed some of it on his palm and then threw back his head and drank thirstily.

He tried not to show how humiliated he felt that these two had seen him fall. Especially Speckles. Flinging away the bottle, Filosofer picked up a child's shovel and scooped up the sand, observing as it ran back down:

'We're between the nursery school and the cemetery. Here there are crappy old nursery teachers, stupid rhymes about little fir-trees growing in woods and disgusting semolina. Over there are graves with worms and crosses eaten away by woodworm. What a bore! And messing around's a bore too. It's time we did something different. What have we sunk to – petty profiteering with cinema tickets.'

'What's profiteering here is private enterprise in America. You said so yourself, Filosofer,' Fantomas cautiously reminded him.

'It's not so much the profiteering I mean, as the scale it's on,' said Filosofer, wrinkling his brow and flinging the child's shovel aside. 'You haven't cottoned on to what I'm saying, Fantomas. It's just that you get big kicks from big business. And what business are you going to be capable of, for instance, Speckles, if you keep whimpering that you can't get yourself a pair of Western-made jeans and go on walking around in some imitation pair from Riga.'

'It's all right for you,' said Speckles, hurt and beginning to justify himself. 'Your father brought you a pair of Wranglers from building the dam in Syria. And as for you, Fantomas, your dad built the port at Nakhodka, and they've got pairs of Levis stacked up there, you said so yourself. But what can my father do?'

'Drop the local accent,' ordered Filosofer with an

50

air of disgust. 'Your old man went and got you a Japanese jacket like ours. So why can't he get you some foreign-label jeans as well. Put the screws on him.'

'I am,' said Speckles, hanging his head. 'But he says to me: "It'd take a whole month's wages to buy a pair of jeans at the market."'

'The jeans themselves aren't the point,' interrupted Filosofer. 'Napoleon didn't wear jeans, but was still Napoleon. And if he'd wanted to, he'd have had a pair. The peoples he conquered would have made them.'

Speckles didn't understand all this about Napoleon, but he sighed.

Filosofer continued:

'As Michurin* said, you shouldn't wait for nature to turn up with the jeans, you've got to go out and get them. It's no good relying on your family, that just makes you weak. Yesterday my old man said to me: "What are you going to do after school?" He's never asked me about anything before, as far as I can remember. All his life he's been up to his ears in cement and concrete, with only his hat sticking out the top. He's got away with handing out presents, these Wranglers for instance. And suddenly he starts taking an interest in his son, while I clam up from the shock of my dad beginning to talk to me. Like in the fable when the fox suddenly starts flattering the crow, "the joy took my breath away". And so my mum gets at my dad in her local committee way, all straight to the point: "And what are you talking to him for, he's brainless, he is!" I dare say she'd shudder if she only knew what I've got in my brains. All my life she's been

---

*Michurin, Russian biologist, 1855–1935

51

comparing me with other boys – all these geniuses at the piano, driven barmy by scales, spotty infant prodigies in maths, creeps in red neckerchiefs howling poetry at Young Pioneer palaces, blockheads from the "skilful fingers" circle, young naturalists stinking of guinea pigs, chess maniacs. "Look at all these clever children around you," she says, "while you're nothing but a dolt." But I've got another talent which our Soviet passion for prodigies just doesn't take into account. I'm a philosopher. Not like the snotty nursery school kid from Omsk that *Literaturnaya Gazeta* went on about, solemnly spouting three-kopeck clichés like "The roots of the sea are an abyss." I am a philosopher of action. It's more interesting to move people about than chess pieces.'

'But move them where?' asked Fantomas, grasping at these enigmatic horizons and sticking another miniature bottle into Filosofer's hand.

'Marie Brizard . . . ' said Filosofer, holding the bottle in the strip of light from the nursery school window and reading the label. His face remained in the dark, however. 'To the other end of the chess board. To where the pawns become queens. Surely, Speckles, you want to become a queen?'

'Yes, I generally . . . well, somehow I . . . yes, I sort of do,' said Speckles in confusion.

'But to become a queen you have to chuck the other pieces off the board,' added Filosofer cruelly.

'Which pieces?' asked Fantomas, breaking out in a sweat in his agitation.

'The ones on the way to becoming queens,' answered Filosofer precisely. 'It's easy to tell the voluntary police patrol by the red armbands they wear. We should set up an anti-police patrol. At first it would be secret. We'd use invisible signs to

52

recognize each other among the red armbands. And then we'd be able to stop hiding when we see that there are a lot of us. From our own families even.'

'But wouldn't we catch it?' asked Speckles in fear.

'We'd catch it if we got scared,' grinned Filosofer. 'We'd need constant training to overcome fear.'

Filosofer sprang from the sand-pit fence, wrapped his legs round the swing frame and began to inch his way up. When he had got to the crossbeam he cried out authoritatively:

'Throw me the rope!'

He put the steel loop back on the hook and leapt off, settling down on the seat again and beginning to swing himself once more.

'So what are we going to do on a fine dark night between the nursery school and the cemetery? I know what! Let's put the two together! After me!' And he dashed from the seat. Empty, it went on swinging for a long time, falling into the strip of light one moment and diving into the darkness the next.

Ardabiev was startled on his way back from Ivan Vesyolykh by seeing the dark outline of a cemetery cross inside the nursery school fence. He shook his head, trying to bring himself to his senses – obviously he had overdone it if such a thing could seem to be.

But after breakfast, when the nursery school teacher, clucking like a sitting hen, led her children out to the sand-pit with their little buckets and spades, she stopped dead in her tracks. A cross from the cemetery, split with age, had been dug right into the middle of the sand-pit. Red cemetery ants, captured with the cross, crawled over the cracks in it. And next to it two miniature bottles rolled in the sand.

# Chapter Three

The orange estate car drew up at the white box of an ordinary Chertanovo block of flats, and Ardabiev junior remembered with despair that the lift had been out of action a whole month. He now had to drag the food and drink for tomorrow's idiotic feast to the seventh floor, all on his own. Bringing the back of the car up to the entrance of the block, he began to unload the provisions on to the pavement under inquisitive and not always approving glances from the pensioners who strolled past the sorry-looking poplars in the yard. The dominoes stopped tapping on a little wooden table in front of the block. Three unremarkable individuals detached themselves from the domino players and walked up, looking in particular, and not without interest, at one of the boxes.

'Need help?' chorused three voices. 'What floor?'

'Thanks,' said Ardabiev, resigning himself to his fate. He had mentally subtracted one bottle from the contents of the box beforehand. 'The seventh.'

'You won't manage it in one go,' said one of the volunteers, scratching his head significantly. He was wearing a checked jersey, blue track-suit trousers with a white trim and for some reason women's slippers with pompoms. But this was his only distinguishing feature. 'Of course if we stacked one box on top of the other . . . ' mused the volunteer. Wheezing, he picked up the box of vodka and nodded at the one containing champagne.

The two others deftly placed the box of champagne

on top. The man with the pompoms sagged slightly from the weight but did not yield. The second volunteer, not without an aggrieved look on his face, lugged the box of soft drinks and the apples. The third took the two buckets, one full of tomatoes, the other of cucumbers. With one hand Ardabiev clasped the three sucking-pigs to his chest, taking with the other the armful of salad stuff, in which the branch of Ardabiola was concealed. Dispiritedly he began to climb the stairs at the tail of the triumphant procession.

At the fourth floor the man with the pompoms let out a grunt and put both boxes down on the landing.

'Time to stop for a smoke,' he said, panting. 'So you're having a wedding reception, are you?'

'No,' answered Ardabiev curtly, and he rested his chin on the pink tail of the top sucking-pig to stop it falling.

'A birthday party?' said the volunteer with the pompoms, refusing to let up.

'No,' answered Ardabiev gloomily. 'It's for getting my thesis accepted.'

'For a doctor's degree?'

'No, a master's.'

'And what's it on, if you don't mind me asking?'

'Ardabiola,' said Ardabiev, who did not usually lie.

'Aha,' said the man with the pompoms, wrinkling his brow thoughtfully.

'Rested enough?' asked Ardabiev.

'Somehow I can't get my breath back. It's a fact I've got high blood pressure. I'm not supposed to lift anything heavy,' explained the helper wearing pompom slippers, looking at the box of vodka.

'While mine's too low,' tittered the second man, carrying the soft drinks and the apples.

'And I get palpitations, the fluttery ones,' added

the third, with the tomatoes and cucumbers.

Ardabiev took the hint.

'The tasting ceremony's on the seventh floor,' he said.

'It's still a long haul to the seventh floor though,' gulped the man in pompom slippers craftily. 'As we're always being told, the historic path is divided into stages. We need to get our strength up.'

'All right,' said Ardabiev, exhausted. 'Get your strength up then.'

'Only you must join us. Come on, it's your thesis after all, not just a load of old tripe!' said the volunteer in pompom slippers, bustling about taking a bottle of vodka out of the box and unscrewing the top.

Seeing that his hands were taken up with the sucking-pigs and salad stuff, the helper put the bottle to Ardabiev's mouth with a slight but gracious bow. Then the hand of one of the other men placed half a cucumber between his teeth in a fatherly gesture. After they had made short work of the bottle the man with the pompoms neatly screwed the top back on and put it back in the empty hole left in the box, restoring the symmetry.

'Come on, fellows! It's nice to help a nice man!'

Surely they can't force their way into my flat as well, can they? thought Ardabiev in a daze, putting the sucking-pigs and salad stuff down in front of his door and deliberately taking a long time to find the key.

'Thank you for your help. I can manage on my own now.'

'Whatever for?' said the man in pompom slippers protectively. 'Once we get down to business we have to finish it off.'

'We have to finish it off!' echoed the second

volunteer, clinking the soft drinks and dropping the apples.

'We'll finish it off! We'll do it in a twinkling!' concluded the third, jangling the buckets of tomatoes and cucumbers.

'And so they will,' thought Ardabiev despairingly, opening the door with a sense of doom. A telegram, flung through the letter box, lay on the rubber mat just beyond the doorway. Ardabiev picked it up and wanted to unfold it, but the box of vodka carried by the helper was pushing him from behind and digging powerfully into his back. He stuck the telegram in his pocket and stood to one side, letting the men into his flat. Their heavy breathing, grunting and conflicting suggestions crowded the flat out as soon as they got inside. The first thing the man with the pompoms did was open the refrigerator, thriftily estimating its contents and capacity.

'Right,' he said thoughtfully. 'I'll throw out this tin of aubergine purée, if you don't mind. It's all like it's broken into blossom. The mayonnaise has gone yellow, get rid of that too. The mustard's dried up – into the bin. The freezer, thank God, is empty. We'll set that aside for the vodka. The tomatoes and cucumbers can go in the boxes at the bottom. But the main thing is to shove the sucking-pigs in. The salad stuff can go down here. The champagne won't go in, which is irritating of it. But we can put it in the bathroom.'

Giving in without complaint, Ardabiev sank on to the divan and unfolded the telegram. It was short. 'Father dead. Funeral Wednesday. Mama.'

'And what about a second little break?' said the man with the pompoms, sitting down next to him on the divan and nudging him playfully in the side. 'Shall

58

we celebrate you getting your master's?'

Ardabiev looked up from the telegram and took in completely unfamiliar people. How did they get into my flat? What do they want? Father's dead – that means Ardabiola was a blind alley. That means everything has failed. And I kidded that girl I was the man of most use to mankind. The funeral's on Wednesday. Why has this character got pompoms on his slippers?

'Get it over with, only fast,' said Ardabiev, sighing out loud.

The man with the pompoms opened another bottle of vodka. The second helper got some glasses out of a glass-fronted cupboard. The third wiped several apples on his sleeve and put them on the table.

'To your master's degree!' exclaimed the volunteer with the pompoms, downing his drink and crunching an apple. 'You're holding us up . . . '

Ardabiev realized that he had a glass in his hand, and also drank.

'Why's she got a face like that, like it's been stretched out?' asked the man with the pompoms, taking an interest in a reproduction Modigliani portrait on the wall.

'Well, she was born with a flat head,' said Ardabiev, resorting to irony, 'so she went and had it lengthened out.'

'They overdid it a bit,' said the man with the pompoms, shaking his head. 'Just what don't they do to people nowadays? And what kind of a bush is this in these boxes of earth?'

'It's for decoration,' answered Ardabiev.

'That's not decorative, surely? Now a little fig-tree, that I can understand. Well now, if you'll just give us the old go-ahead – to your doctor's degree!' Suddenly,

59

however, the volunteer with the pompoms choked and froze where he was sitting.

Ardabiev looked up and saw his wife standing in the middle of the room. That is, not his wife any more, because they had separated. But all the same she was still his wife, because they had not yet divorced. None of the things in the flat were hers, but she still had a second key.

Her beautiful suede shoes with white stitching had trodden on the branch of Ardabiola, which had been dropped in the confusion. But Ardabiev did not care now.

The men withered immediately under her sarcastic gaze and withdrew, one after the other. The one with the pompoms went out on tiptoes.

'Are these new friends of yours?' Ardabiev's wife asked him, sitting down and lighting a cigarette. The mocking expression remained in her eyes but she jabbed at the lighter nervously, unconfidently.

'Aha,' said Ardabiev. 'Brand new.'

'And where indeed is your friend Alla? The cage is empty. She hasn't left you as well, has she?'

'She passed away.'

'One usually talks of a rat dying.'

'She passed away.'

'All right, you can have it your way. You always were humane towards animals. No one will take that away from you. I'm sorry I came without calling first. There was no answer. I wanted to congratulate you on your thesis. I heard you were inviting people round tomorrow. A lot of people don't realize we're living apart, you know. And I thought . . . '

'What did you think?' asked Ardabiev, lifting the branch of Ardabiola from the floor and turning it in his hands.

'I'm not pushing to be invited – I thought the flat would probably be in a mess. I wanted to give you a hand. But it's all clean. Is someone helping you?'

'No.'

'Well done. And have you had the sense to buy anything?'

'Yes.'

She went over to the refrigerator and looked inside it:

'You're making progress as a housewife, Ardabiev, you've even got some sucking-pigs. Who's going to roast them?'

'Have you got your driving licence with you?' asked Ardabiev.

'Yes, I have. Why do you ask?'

'Could you take me to Domodedovo Airport then, and look after my guests tomorrow. Do help me out. I haven't got time to ring and make apologies.'

'What?' she asked, and stood rooted by the open refrigerator door.

'My father's dead.'

She made an involuntary movement towards him, but restrained herself.

'When? What happened to him?'

'You'll take me then?'

She went to the wardrobe, took out two shirts, underwear and socks, and again it struck her that everything was clean and pressed.

When she went into the bathroom to get his razor, before she noticed the stack of champagne bottles in the water, she saw two shirts hanging up to dry on wooden coat hangers, and pants and socks on the radiator, and realized that Ardabiev was doing his own washing. She wanted to burst into tears, both because of this and because his father had died. But she did not cry, merely took the razor and another pair of socks which were dry to the touch.

For some time they drove in silence.

'Have you ever thought that you too will die?' she asked, turning on the side-lights as it was getting dark.

'Yes, I have. I don't want it to happen right now. I don't have any right to die. There is a lot I haven't managed to do yet,' said Ardabiev gloomily.

'But can you think of even one man in history who managed to get everything done?' she asked, lighting another cigarette. 'No one has managed to do everything before dying. Christ did not manage to make all men brothers. Hitler did not manage to thrust all the Jews into the gas-chambers. Your father did not manage to see his grandson, whom I killed within me without your permission. And I have also died, because I have not managed to become a mother.'

'Don't torment yourself,' said Ardabiev, sinking his head into his shoulders.

'I killed your child because I loved you,' she continued. 'I felt the child would get in your way. I wanted you to get your thesis accepted, to stand on your own two feet. But you couldn't forgive me. You stopped talking to me. You didn't tell me anything, not even why a rat came to live in the canary's cage, nor about your father having cancer. You thought I had fallen out of love with you. But can you imagine that there is a kind of love for which you would kill your own child? Why did you come to hate me?'

'I didn't come to hate you. I couldn't forget it,' said Ardabiev, sighing heavily. He was thinking about the girl in the cap: why had she too done the same thing?

'You don't have to hurt me any more, Ardabiev. I am punished by the fact that I love you and no one else.' And quietly she asked him, in a faltering voice that was on the verge of breaking: 'Tell me, will you ever be able to forget? To forgive me?'

'I don't know,' answered Ardabiev, and fell silent. He said no more until they got to the airport. Only as he opened the door of the orange car did he say: 'There's no need to tell the guests about my father's death. Think up another reason for me not being there. Something funny so they'll be cheerful. Don't forget – I haven't invited the Mishechkins.'

'And what if they gatecrash?' she asked, wiping away her tears, but speaking in a different tone of voice now.

# Chapter Four

Ardabiev walked across the airfield behind a crowd of passengers. In his left hand he carried his only luggage – a briefcase he had brought back from Africa, with a tiny lizard-like crocodile sewn into the skin of another crocodile, which in life had probably been a little bigger. The baby crocodile's claws dangled over the lock on the case. With his right hand, Ardabiev clasped a sleeping boy of about two years old to his chest. The child's hand round Ardabiev's neck gripped a toy moon-mobile tenaciously and its antenna tickled the back of his head. The little boy looked as if he had climbed out of the picture on a packet of baby food. He had white curls like wood shavings, a crafty turned-up nose and such tight round cheeks that each seemed to have an apple underneath it. His mother walked next to Ardabiev, a tiny baby in a snow-white bundle in her arms. A string bag stuffed with oranges hung from her elbow, bumping against her leg as she walked. One of the holes in the string bag had torn open, and several fallen oranges formed a dotted line which marked out her route across the airfield.

Just an hour earlier Ardabiev had been desperately thrusting the telegram reporting his father's death at the official in charge of the transport service. This was a man with brutal but persecuted eyes – eyes that had grown dull looking at the hands stretched out to him, holding other telegrams, business trip notification letters and special little red passes of various kinds, printed in gold, red and other colours. Flights to the Soviet far east and Siberia had been cancelled for two days and hundreds of people were sleeping on benches or simply on the floor. Ardabiev's telegram had not helped. At Domodedovo Airport they had got used to the fact that someone dies somewhere every day. When the flight schedule for two days before was finally announced, Ardabiev opened up his telegram and, holding it out, walked slowly along the queue to the check-in desk. Most of the people turned their backs. All of them had business matters – deaths too, perhaps.

'Wait a moment.' Suddenly a voice rang out and Ardabiev saw a young army captain with little cannons on his collar tabs. His face was covered with two days' growth of golden stubble, but his eyes were clear and humane.

In his arms the captain held a sleeping child, who was refusing to let go the toy moon-mobile even in his sleep. Next to the captain stood his wife, shyly breast-feeding the child's younger brother.

'This is the second time you've gone past us with your telegram,' said the captain. 'My wife and I were wondering – would you be able to take on this Red Skin Chief?' and he nodded at the sleeping child in his arms.

'I could try,' said Ardabiev. 'But you've got two of them.'

'That's all right, I'll take another flight,' said the captain. 'I've got two days of my holiday left. And you can fly with my wife and children. A father dies only once in a lifetime.'

Ardabiev turned to look at the captain's wife. He was prepared for anything, but not for the smile she gave him. She smiled, instinctively covering her breast

66

with her hand and gently rocking the baby. There was even some guilt in her smile, as if she, her husband and children were somehow to blame for his father's death and for his not having a ticket.

'Have you got your passport?' said the captain, hurrying Ardabiev. 'We must get on with transferring the ticket.'

While the officials were reallocating the ticket, suspiciously checking Ardabiev's face and the captain's against their documents – completely incapable of understanding why the same child was being entered on a ticket made out in a different name – the captain gave Ardabiev his instructions:

'Bear in mind that Vitya is only a little angel when he's asleep. He's frightful once he's awake. It's perpetual motion. Be on guard all the time. Indeed he'll only be waiting for the grown-ups to turn their backs. Yesterday he stuck his fingers down his grandmother's mincer and was just about to turn the handle. He'll give you a really hard time of it. It's quite possible he'll try to seize the plane. I don't envy you. Can you change nappies?'

'No,' admitted Ardabiev honestly.

'You'll have to learn. He only says "potty" once he's already gone. All in all it's a matter of your rescuing me, not the other way round.'

That was why Ardabiev found himself on the airfield with someone else's child. This was the first child he had ever held in his arms. He had been the youngest in his family and hadn't had to lug his little brothers around. He carried this child that was not his own and thought of how he could have been carrying one that was.

He also thought about the girl in the cap.

A crowd of overwrought passengers massed on the

tarmac, as if the aeroplane would fly off at any minute leaving someone behind on the airfield. It simply did not enter anyone's head that there were exactly as many seats in the plane as there were passengers. All their thoughts narrowed down to a driving anxiety to get in, made more intense by a fear of not being able to. The crush was nonsensical, but it did not let up.

Seeing the two children, a stewardess with a face like a boxer bellowed:

'Make way for passengers with children! Show some sense!'

But no one shifted their elbows, bags or boxes out of the way.

The stewardess kicked a cardboard box with one foot and someone's double-bass case with the other. The box was marked with the black symbols of a glass and an umbrella, and a clinking noise issued from within it. She stood up at the bottom of the steps, screening the aeroplane with her mighty body, and dismissed the sticky, crumpled tickets held out to her with a flick of the hand.

'Passengers with children first!'

Seeing that they were not going to get round the stewardess, the passengers grudgingly made way, giving Ardabiev with the sleeping child and the mother holding the tiny baby such unfriendly looks that the unseasonable weather and all other earthly misfortunes – large and small – might have been created by them.

'Why are people so embittered?' sighed the mother. She settled the baby on her knees, put the string bag of oranges under her seat and went off to sleep immediately.

She had a simple broad Russian face with heavy plaits, the colour of corn, done up in a bun on her head.

They're not all embittered, thought Ardabiev with relief. Both she and her husband, with young children into the bargain, had suffered two days and nights of hell at the airport, no less than the others. But they hadn't become bitter. They had understood what the words 'father dead' meant on a telegram. And the stewardess with the boxer-like face, although she was worn out too, had understood what it means to have children in your arms. But why was there so much loutishness, so much shoving and elbowing? Why had they got so brutish? Life is not easy but surely that is no excuse? Why should one make a hard life harder still? We must never forget that we are people, human beings.

The child on his knees slept soundly, and Ardabiev also tried to fall asleep to the even rumble of the airborne plane. He rarely dreamt, but merely had to close his eyes for scenes made up of confused fragments from his life to cluster in front of him. So now, perhaps because he had by chance touched the two rough little claws of the tiny crocodile on his briefcase, Ardabiev began to remember.

A narrow boat, hollowed out of a single tree, moved across a lake. An African gently plied his oars among the stars that swam in the black water. He wore an electric lamp like a miner's on his forehead and swept the ray of light that shone from it along the thickets on the bank and over the water. It seemed as if a white star had grown on the African's head. Suddenly two green eyes began to burn in the mud on the bank, caught by the ray of light. Dropping his oars the African grabbed a wooden spear with an iron tip and made a strong and agile movement. The body of a tiny crocodile with a delicate white underbelly soared up on the tip of the spear in the ray of light. The crocodile sobbed like a child. The African threw it into the bottom of the boat and struck its head with a hammer. The crocodile fell silent. The African wiped the blood off the spear point with a rag and got it ready for the next pair of green eyes.

'Don't!' Ardabiev said to him in English.

'But it was you who wanted to watch a crocodile hunt, wasn't it?' asked the African, astonished.

'I've seen enough,' said Ardabiev. 'I didn't realize they'd be so small.'

'There aren't many large crocodiles in this lake,' said the African. 'There aren't many of them generally. But we make ladies' handbags and briefcases out of these little ones.'

'Don't you think it's a shame?' asked Ardabiev.

'It's my job,' said the African, shrugging his shoulders. 'I don't kill the hens myself, for instance. My wife does it. But what kind of hunting do you have in Russia? I've heard you've got tigers and bears there.'

'There are still some left,' said Ardabiev, sighing. 'But there are fewer and fewer of them.'

'One day man won't be there either,' said the African. 'People are the only animals that hunt each other. Not even hyenas do that. Do you know what animals think about us? They think they're the people, while people are the animals.'

Gradually Ardabiev went off to sleep, clasping the strange child to him, and for once had a dream.

Ardabiev was telephoning the girl in the cap from his empty flat, in front of the empty cage, no longer inhabited by Alla the rat, who had passed away. Suddenly he felt something behind him – a stare. He turned round. A man stood there, having got in goodness knows how. He had the face of all the aeroplane passengers put together, not wanting to let the children through to the plane. On his feet were ladies' slippers with pompoms on them.

'There's no point in ringing,' said the man. 'The lines have been cut.'

Other people began coming into the room after him, also with faces like the passengers, and all wearing slippers with pompoms. One of them opened a double-bass case, in which lay a dismantled rifle with a telescopic sighting device. He began to put it together, squirting it with sewing-machine oil from a shiny can. A second man undid a cardboard box marked with a glass and an umbrella, and took out several cartridges. The others opened the refrigerator, took out a tiny murdered crocodile and began to eat it raw, tearing off its claws and spitting out the skin, like pineapple peel, on to the floor. Once they had eaten the crocodile they began to move towards Ardabiev, with hard, still hungry eyes. Ardabiev wanted to cry out, but he could not. He woke up in a cold sweat, and saw to his joy, in place of the terrible eyes of the murderers clustering round him, the clear eyes of the child which was not, but seemed to be, his own. The little boy was looking with curiosity now at Ardabiev, now at the briefcase, on which the crocodile's claws dangled. Tentatively the child put his fingers between the crocodile's teeth, but it did not bite.

'Good morning, Vitya!' said Ardabiev, although it was still night.

'Potty,' said Vitya and, remembering the father's instructions, Ardabiev looked inquiringly round at the mother, but she was deeply and evenly asleep. 'Potty,' repeated Vitya insistently.

What on earth should I do? thought Ardabiev feverishly.

He got up with Vitya in his arms and went to the lavatory. With two of them in there it was cramped and uncomfortable. Ardabiev put Vitya on the edge of the washbasin and began taking off his trousers, getting muddled up with the straps and buttons. There was a nappy under the trousers. Raising Vitya's bottom to his face, Ardabiev sniffed at it. It didn't seem to smell of anything. Vitya, who had only been pretending to keep quiet, managed at this moment to grab a bottle of floral toilet water from the washstand and drop it on the floor with a crash, covering it with a mass of glass splinters.

'Now what did you do that for, Vitya?' asked Ardabiev reproachfully.

'Potty,' he replied.

Ardabiev drew back his nappy and carefully tucked a hand down it. The nappy was dry.

'Well done, Vitya,' said Ardabiev. 'And I thought you only signalled "potty" after the event. Now then, let's try and get down to work.' Ardabiev unwound the nappy, hung it neatly over the towel and lifted Vitya on to the lavatory bowl.

'Come on, grunt, Vitya,' said Ardabiev. 'It helps.'

Perplexed, Vitya looked at Ardabiev, not understanding him.

'Like this,' said Ardabiev, and began to demonstrate.

Vitya understood and also began to grunt assiduously, screwing up his eyes with pleasure at the new sounds being elicited from him.

First of all a fine transparent stream began to flow from his little pink tap, falling not into the lavatory bowl, but straight on to Ardabiev's jeans.

'A good start, Vitya,' said Ardabiev, encouraging his efforts. 'Now let's turn to more serious business.

Close ranks and take action. The whole world is watching you.'

Vitya understood the gravity of the historic moment and took action. Something plopped into the lavatory bowl.

'Well done, Vitya!' said Ardabiev, evaluating his work. 'The peoples of the world applaud you!'

Ardabiev washed Vitya's plump little bottom, dried it with lavatory paper, and began to roll him up awkwardly in his nappy. Having somehow completed this complicated process, Ardabiev put his trousers back on, did up the straps and suddenly saw to his horror that Vitya was thoughtfully eating the soap, which he had seized from the washstand.

'That can't taste nice, surely, Vitya?' he said, shaking his head and taking it away.

Vitya let out a deafening yell, unhappy at this interruption of his heart's desire. The lavatory door had already been tugged at several times, ever more insistently.

'Won't be long,' Ardabiev called out in dismay, prising Vitya from the box of lavatory paper which he had begun to hurl in the air with barbaric shrieks.

Ardabiev got down on his knees and swept up the splinters of glass into the lavatory paper, suffocating from the nauseating flowery smell. Once up he was only just in time to pull Vitya out of the lavatory bowl, into which he had, out of curiosity, tried to thrust his angelic blond little head. The door was being rattled now, not tugged at. Opening it with Vitya in his arms, Ardabiev squeezed with difficulty through the queue now shifting from leg to leg. As Vitya kicked out furiously in the gangway, his sandal knocked the glasses off the nose of a man engrossed in a copy of *Health Magazine*.

73

'It's disgraceful!' cried the man, flying into a rage and only just managing to pull his glasses from under Ardabiev's feet in time. 'Children shouldn't be allowed to fly! Aeroflot isn't a nursery school!'

Ardabiev only had to put Vitya down on the ground for him to skilfully wriggle his hand free and tear headlong down the gangway, running into a fragile stewardess who was dispensing soft drinks. Plastic cups flew off in different directions, spraying lemonade on dresses and jackets, while the metal tray crashed down sideways right on to the cardboard box marked with the glass and umbrella, which rested on the lap of a lady in a light blue wig. A plaintive crunch came from inside the box.

'My Czech dinner service!' she cried out, feverishly untying the string round the box.

And at that moment, fascinated by the sight of it, Vitya got his little hands into the gleaming wig and tugged it powerfully towards him. It came away easily and smoothly, like a light blue puff of smoke, revealing scanty wisps of hair beneath. The lady lost her voice, and only a spluttering escaped her lips, as if she was having the air let out of her.

Ardabiev tried to seize the wig from Vitya, but the little boy had got a tight hold on it and was waving it like a trophy, letting out warlike cries.

'Give aunty back her toy,' the stewardess gently asked Vitya, and to Ardabiev's surprise he immediately obeyed.

When Ardabiev collapsed exhausted back in his seat with Vitya, the latter began to take an interest in his shaven head and started scratching it with his small but sharp nails.

'I'm a hedgehog,' said Ardabiev, 'I can prick you,' and he butted Vitya.

74

Vitya liked this, and he butted Ardabiev back. Peacefully they carried on butting each other. But Ardabiev only had to turn his back for Vitya to pull his sleeping brother's ear. The baby gave a heart-rending cry and his mother woke and smacked Vitya gently. Vitya took umbrage and also began to yell. The outcome was a deafening duet.

'There's no need to smack us,' Ardabiev told Vitya's mother. 'We've just done both number one and number two. Our nappy is dry because we didn't just go anywhere, but in the public lavatory.'

'Incredible,' said their mother, feeling Vitya's nappy in disbelief. 'No doubt you've got small children too.'

'No,' said Ardabiev, lowering his head, 'I haven't.'

'Are you married, though?' she couldn't resist asking.

He didn't give her an answer.

All of a sudden the aeroplane shook, once and then again.

'Slight turbulence, please fasten your seatbelts!' said the stewardess sweetly.

But Ardabiev felt her sweetness concealed menace.

'Don't fall, aeroplane, don't,' begged Ardabiev in silence, closing his eyes. 'There are many good people on board, as well as the secret of Ardabiola. Perhaps my father didn't die of cancer? Perhaps Ardabiola is a great discovery all the same?'

And the aeroplane seemed to obey, and righted itself.

# Chapter Five

Today at the Khairiuzovsk depot, the metal-workers' hammers were somehow more muted in their pounding. Even the welding machines hissed with more restraint than usual, trying to temper the fireworks of white sparks, and the engines crawled in and out more quietly and slowly. A coffin, covered with a piece of red cloth with a black border, lay under the soot-blackened brick arches of the depot. It rested on an old hand-trolley under which the rails glinted. Without downing their tools, the day-shift workers were going up to the manager and he was fastening red and black armbands to the grease-stained sleeves of their overalls. They stood in the guard of honour, then returned to their engines, and the iron music of their tools blended with the funereal tunes of the railway brass band. Death did not interrupt work, and work treated death with respect. Today no one used strong language at the depot, and no one smoked by the red bucket of sand. The working class of the Khairiuzovsk railway had asked the widow for such a funeral and she had appreciated their request.

Andrei Ivanovich Ardabiev's face was so locked in concentration that it seemed as if he were driving his engine once more, only with his eyes closed, as if blind. Had he wanted, he could probably have done this in his lifetime. Beneath him once again were the rails, which had given him sure and loyal service. He was dressed in his woollen suit for special occasions, a white shirt and a tie with blue spots on it, tied for the first time by someone else. The striped corner of a handkerchief could be seen beneath his folded arms. The photographer on the local paper was there, short with a small bluish nose. He had taken pictures of Andrei Ivanovich many times while alive, and had come to carry out his final duty and photograph him dead. He did this, not for the newspaper, where they only printed pictures of living exemplary workers, but for himself. He photographed the coffin and the workers in the guard of honour by lying on the rails and almost sticking his lens into their hands, gripping files and chisels. The wide-angle lens lengthened these hands like an El Greco but made their heads smaller, stretching them high up somewhere under the Gothic-like arches of the depot. No one laughed at the photographer crawling about the rails, because they all understood he was working. Andrei Ivanovich's widow sat on a simple office chair, oddly out of place next to the rails. When she raised a handkerchief to her eyes to wipe away her tears, the photographer started. His frame caught the two handkerchiefs, the one in the woman's trembling fingers and the one behind the dead man's arms. He had only a moment to decide on which handkerchief to focus. He chose the handkerchief behind the dead man's arms, but the one held by the widow was also visible in the frame, although it was not so sharp. A splendid shot, thought the photographer, clicking the shutter with lightning speed. It must be called *Two Handkerchiefs*. But who'll exhibit it? And he too felt in his pocket for his own handkerchief to wipe away the tears that dimmed the viewfinder. Oh Andrei Ivanovich, Andrei Ivanovich – a beautiful send-off, but better you were alive. Thus did the photographer record the funeral – through his tears.

Against the hand-trolley bearing the coffin lay wreaths of paper flowers on wire – from the depot, the local Party executive committee and the district committee. Taiga *zharki*, wild daisies and bright scarlet geraniums cut from pots had been brought by friends and neighbours and placed by the coffin and inside it. There were branches of cedar with dark heavy cones. And the former metal-worker Ivan Vesyolykh, now a pensioner, had brought velvety dark red dahlias, which he had cut in broad daylight from a flower bed on the station square. He had not gone to see Yesenin. A scarlet cushion bearing Andrei Ivanovich's medals lay between his feet: *For Victory over Germany, For the Defence of Moscow, For the Capture of Berlin* and *For Bravery*, along with his *Order of the Red Banner of Labour*. The photographer remembered the words of the song, '. . . and on his chest gleamed a medal for the city of Budapest', although Andrei Ivanovich did not have a medal for liberating Budapest.

Behind the seated widow stood two of her sons, their hands on her quivering shoulders. The oldest was a surgeon who had flown from the far north and the middle one was the police inspector in charge of the Irkutsk sobering-up station, both like their father to look at, with high foreheads and broad cheekbones. The youngest son, a Moscow biologist, had not arrived, although they had sent him a telegram. New people came and the depot grew more and more crowded: old Siberian women in black plush jackets, elderly men with sticks who had known Andrei Ivanovich's father, greasers, engine-drivers, electricians, the women who worked the points, signalmen, young people from the railway school and waitresses from the station restaurant.

79

'Shall we start the civil ceremony?' asked Pestrukhin, bending obligingly over the widow.

'Do what you want,' she answered.

And Pestrukhin took a piece of paper out of his breast pocket, straightened his shoulders and began to talk so cheerfully that his speech might have been about awarding a medal to a live man, not burying a dead one.

The widow did not hear these words, but looked at the face which would soon be covered with the coffin lid for ever. Then she felt another pair of hands on her shoulder, and without looking round knew that they were the hands of her youngest son.

When the trolley moved off down the rails with the coffin, the engines standing at the depot – and all the local junctions – began to hoot in unison, as if to swamp the words which had just been uttered, and this wail was picked up by the Moscow-Vladivostok train which had just moved away from the platform.

The coffin was lifted off the trolley and carried on straps by six railway workers. Two railway workers followed close by, bearing the red coffin lid on their heads – one could not tell whether or not they were crying underneath it. The ground was all either of them could see to stop them stumbling. The sons took their mother's arms and led her behind the coffin lid. Her legs had swollen up completely now and refused to obey her. They were followed by a crowd of people, perhaps a thousand strong, perhaps two thousand strong, who understand that the death of each working person deserves the same respect as does his life. When they took the coffin out into the station square and put it on the open lorry, the drivers of the dilapidated Khairiuzovsk taxis, standing to attention outside their cars, put their right hands on their steering wheels and pressed their horns, all at the same time, continuing the wail of the engines which had just subsided. Up in the back of the lorry with the coffin, the photographer suddenly saw that the small silver-painted statue of Lenin had merged in the wide-angle lens with the body of Andrei Ivanovich, as if he were holding a little figure between his folded arms. The photographer just managed to take the shot, despite the jolt of the lorry moving off. He thought of how Lenin had made the revolution for such people as Andrei Ivanovich, and of how the old engine-driver did not want to give Lenin up into others' hands, even in death.

As she sat in the lorry next to the coffin, the widow looked at her husband going on his last journey, and felt still more terrified by the way his hair stirred in the wind as if alive, while he himself was dead. The three sons sat next to her, and all three were like their father. The youngest son gripped the briefcase made with the tiny African crocodile, which could never have foretold that it would find its way from its own waters almost to Lake Baikal itself.

The youngest Ardabiev had nearly been too late for the funeral because bad weather had kept him in Omsk for two days. He had made friends with Vitya, who had contrived to bring him a dozen carefully selected cigarette ends in a panama hat, and to tear the arms and legs off a plastic doll belonging to a little girl passenger whose plaits he had also nearly pulled off. He had thrown a bottle of milk down some stairs, pushed himself nearly half-way through the iron railings of a balcony and licked out half a jar of shoe polish pinched from an airport bootblack. However, to make up for all this he had done both number one and number two, and only in the public lavatory,

balanced in Ardabiev's arms. They had parted in
Irkutsk, and in farewell Vitya had given Ardabiev his
moon-mobile – minus one of its antennae by then.

The railway brass band following the coffin continued to play, and without his mother hearing,
Ardabiev was able to whisper to his eldest brother,
the surgeon:

'What did he die of?'

The brother answered, also in a whisper: 'He had a
lot to drink. At his old friend's, Ivan Vesyolykh. He
came in late and lay down without undressing. He
just took his boots off. And he never woke up in the
morning.'

'Was there a post-mortem?' asked the youngest son
quickly.

'I insisted on one. It took place in my presence.
There had been no haemorrhage in either heart or
brain. A heart attack's been ruled out. The other
doctors and I were completely baffled.'

'And his lungs? Did you see any secondaries in his
lungs?'

'No, we didn't. How would he have got secondaries?
Where did you get that idea from? It's true some
residual scarring was noted, but it was barely noticeable. It wasn't even scarring, just slight hardening. It
might have been an insignificant congenital defect
perhaps. He died a completely healthy man.'

'So there were no secondaries?' gasped the youngest
Ardabiev with emotion.

'I told you there weren't. How long are you going
to keep on about one and the same thing? Why are
you beaming for joy next to your dead father? What
difference does it make if there were secondaries or
not, if he's dead?' said the surgeon brother, frowning.

'But what did he die of then?' asked the youngest

82

son, seizing hold of his brother's sleeve, his eyes burning with excitement.

'What's the matter with you? You sound feverish.'

'What did he die of?' begged the youngest Ardabiev, beginning to shake him.

'I couldn't make it out at all. When the trachea was opened up it was blocked with a thin, soup-like liquid. Something had taken place that was terrible in its absurdity. Like a child he must have been sick in his sleep, and the vomit got into the respiratory tract. All he needed to do was clear his throat, and everything would have been all right.'

'He didn't have any secondaries. That means the Ardabiola worked!' whispered the youngest son, and he burst into tears.

He cried both from grief, that his father had died such a crazy death, and from happiness, that he, his son, would now be able to help so many people on earth not to die.

'What is Ardabiola? Are you delirious or something?' asked the eldest son anxiously.

'Tell me, haven't you got used to people dying?' the youngest brother asked him. 'You're a surgeon, after all. You've cut up both the living and the dead so many times.'

'A doctor doesn't have any right to get used to death. If you get used to it you should get out of medicine,' answered the eldest son. 'Do you know what the Evenki* people do at their funerals? They break the dead man's gun, his skis and sledge, they smash his crockery and his mirror, tear his clothes into shreds and throw everything into the grave. In

---

* An ethnic group of north-east Siberia.

doing this they indicate that things have no meaning without man.'

'Another taxi-driver was killed in our area a week ago,' said the police inspector, the middle son, entering into the conversation. 'They threw a telephone lead round his neck from behind and strangled him. We caught two youths, all but kids still. And you know what they said? "We didn't have enough money for a cassette player." So there's someone who murders for gain for you. Why have material possessions taken on more importance than men for many people? The shortages? Rubbish! A shortage of feeling – that's what it is. But where on earth does it come from? We've got everything right it seems, and we've begun to live better. But in the police we sometimes see such things that even we are horrified – what has made us like this? Doctors shouldn't get used to death, and surely we shouldn't either. I see it like this – diseases are killers, but killers are diseases too. They're not just individual sick people but diseases, with all that that entails. Sometimes when I'm on duty at the sobering-up station I get seized by such depression. Then I pick up Mayakovsky's poems and read. There are drunken mugs all around me, but I am reading Mayakovsky . . . '

To the funeral music of the brass band, the middle brother quoted in a whisper:

> 'A poor honour would it be
> Should graven images of me rise from such roses
> Over squares where consumption spits
> Where there are hooligans and whores and
> syphilis . . .

'I see it like this: we've dealt with consumption, it seems. As regards whores and syphilis – we're managing, even if we have got a way to go. But the hooligan has flourished. At first, I thought, as one does in the sobering-up station, that vodka's the cause. It is, partly. But only partly. It's a void of feeling that's to blame. This void is the tuberculosis of the soul. It's the consumption we still haven't learnt how to cure.'

'Mayakovsky applied to a chemist,' remembered the surgeon brother, 'for a workshop for raising men from the dead. But no one can be raised from the dead, can they? Not Mayakovsky, nor my Evenki, nor our father. Nor us, when we die.'

'How do you know?' asked the youngest Ardabiev. 'If a yogi can lie on a bed of nails, then so can everyone else. All you need is to know how to concentrate. If old Abkhazian men can live until they're a hundred and fifty, then everyone can live to a hundred and fifty. You just have to know how to live. We still know very little about ourselves and our powers. First of all we must learn not to be ill. And then we must learn not to die.'

'And learn not to kill,' said the middle brother, sticking to his theme. 'I see it like this: while there's hooliganism, people will go on knifing each other. And while people go on knifing each other, there'll be war. War, that's also a disease. That's how I see it.'

Suddenly all three brothers froze and half got up, peering forward over the cab of the lorry. An identical lorry with black and red sides and a coffin in the back was winding along the street towards them. The coffin was also followed by a brass band, its battered trumpets gleaming, and a crowd shuffled along behind. Another widow sat next to the coffin in the back of the lorry, only she was so young that there could not have been three grown-up sons next to her.

The lorry was moving in the opposite direction to the old Khairiuzovsk cemetery, towards the new one, laid out for the industrial complex builders.

The photographer knew who was lying in this coffin. The lock on the safety harness worn by a twenty-year-old construction worker had failed, and he had fallen on to the sharp steel spikes that were to reinforce the concrete. The photographer had heard this discussed at an emergency meeting when a trainee reporter from Irkutsk, her eyes blazing with righteous anger, had offered to write an article criticizing the safety devices used at the site. The editor, concealing from her his eyes which never burned with anything, had told her gently: 'Isn't it a bit early for you to take on a topic like this, Semenkina?' He was hoping for a flat in one of the construction workers' breeze-block buildings.

The two funeral tunes played by the two brass bands going in their opposite directions blended into one. The lorries drew alongside each other, bearing the coffins of two men who had not known each other in their lifetimes, and the photographer clicked the shutter at the very moment that the two widows – one old, one young – looked up at each other, their eyes dimmed with tears. Who needs this picture? thought the photographer. For I'll die too one day, and with me my negatives. But he suppressed these bitter thoughts and furiously began to photograph all the things that he could never hope to print or put on show: the depot workers carrying the tin memorial obelisk with its red star, as they slid around on the wet cemetery clay, the widow's hands, which she had slipped, twitching, into the chink between the lid and the coffin, through which the dead man's face was still visible; the pensioner Ivan Vesyolykh, using an axe-head to drive large nails which kept bending into the coffin; the coffin being lowered on ropes pulled taut into the gaping womb of earth; handfuls of grain flying into the grave from the palms of the old women; clods of earth leaping from spades; proletarian hands each taking a pinch of rice and raisin kasha from the enamel bowl placed on the fresh grave mound.

Ivan Vesyolykh came up to the youngest son and knocked against his shoulder. His face, withered and old, like a child's fist to look at, wrinkled up and he began to tremble.

'I'm to blame for everything. I'm . . . He stayed too long at my place. I was the one who was going to die, and I've gone and pulled him with me.'

The widow took the little broom made of twigs, given to her according to custom, and swept the edge of the grave mound. Then although this was not easy for her either, she bowed down from her waist to the people assembled there:

'And now Andrei Ivanovich invites you to partake . . .'

The photographer managed to get a photograph of her low bow, and when he realized that he had got through all his film he began to weep, no longer fearing that his tears would cloud the view-finder.

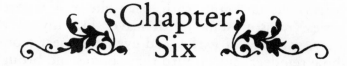

# Chapter Six

Andrei Ivanovich had invited many guests; indeed he
was the only person not to turn up. Tables covered
with white tablecloths and laid for fifty people stood
along three walls of the largest room. The tablecloths
had come both from the Ardabievs' house and from
the neighbours: some with tassels, some with lace,
some embroidered with cross-stitch, others with
satin-stitch. The tables under the cloths were also
both from the house itself and from the neighbours:
some oak, some mahogany, some just plain kitchen
tables and even one taken from the school staff room.
The guests sat mainly on stools with boards wrapped
in newspaper laid on top of them. The plates with
little flowers belonged to the family, while those with
rather worn, gilded edges came from the depot
canteen, along with the aluminium forks that bent.
One thing though was the same for all the guests: the
little cut glasses designed to hold a hundred grams of
vodka each.

Andrei Ivanovich was a generous host, treating
them to meat in aspic that quivered gravely under
their knives, his own slightly salted cucumbers with
blackcurrant leaves sticking to their warty sides,
make-believe toadstools made of hard-boiled eggs and
tomatoes cut in half, egg-shells stuffed with mashed
up egg yolk and sprinkled with dill, shining silver

*khairiuzi*, sauerkraut with bead-like red whortle-berries, ramson stalks with leaves like lily of the valley, smelling of garlic, and even the meat from a whole reindeer, cut up into three boxes and brought on the plane by Andrei Ivanovich's eldest son from the far-off lands of the Evenki. But when it came to the vodka, Andrei Ivanovich allowed only three glasses each. After this the guests had to get up and leave their seats for the others waiting their turn in the yard. The only ones who did not have to move were the widow and her three sons.

'Welcome,' said the widow, smiling at the first fifty guests. 'Come and pay your respects to Andrei Ivanovich.'

When they got up she said, also with a smile:

'Come for forty days. Andrei Ivanovich will be expecting you.'

The old Khairiuzovsk women, taciturn and noise-less as ghosts, managed in an instant to change all the plates, knives and forks so that the new shift could sit down at a freshly laid table.

'Welcome,' said the widow, smiling at the second fifty guests. 'Come and pay your respects to Andrei Ivanovich!'

And when they got up, she said, still with a smile:

'Come for forty days. Andrei Ivanovich will be expecting you.'

And three times did the widow smile and say 'welcome', and three times did the plates change on the table, and three times did she remind them happily that Andrei Ivanovich would expect them for forty days.

But the fourth and last shift were Andrei Ivano-

90

vich's closest friends, and the widow no longer had to tell them 'welcome', but sighed deeply and looked around her:

'Well, thank God we don't have to hurry any more. Andrei Ivanovich didn't like hurrying over his meals.'

'You know what mother said to me when I arrived?' whispered the eldest Ardabiev to the youngest one. 'She drank a glass of vodka, struck the table with her fist and said: "Now no one will be able to take him away from me." There's a woman for you.'

The eldest brother cast a sidelong glance at the middle one.

'And what are you up to, Inspector, not drinking at all, like some fair maiden?'

The latter felt embarrassed:

'I gave up when they sent me to work in the sobering-up station. Do you know what particularly struck me the first time I went on duty? I opened the door and it was all dark in there, except that in the strip of light from the door you could see naked feet sticking out on plank beds. And on the toes were curling nails, ingrowing and crooked, like the claws of wild beasts. Then and there I remembered, "'Man' is a word with a proud ring to it". So I gave up drinking completely.'

'An idealist in a policeman's uniform,' smiled the surgeon brother indulgently. 'But when you're doing an operation in a tent and it's fifty degrees below zero, you can't get by without a mouthful of alcohol. Your hands wouldn't be able to hold the scalpel. You know, I'm already beginning to rather miss my Evenki people.' To his astonishment the eldest son realized he had lapsed into the local Siberian accent: 'Hey, listen to that! I slipped into the old way of speaking. It's my blood beginning to talk.'

'May I read you a poem?' asked Ivan Vesyolykh, tottering as he got up, with a crumpled piece of paper torn out of a school exercise book and scribbled all over with indelible pencil. 'I wrote it right there at the cemetery. After hammering the nails in . . . '

'Read it out,' said the widow. 'Only don't drink any more.'

His face contorted with emotion and guilt, Ivan Vesyolykh began to read, brandishing the sheet of paper:

'Farewell, Andrei Ivanych,
Railman of Siberia.
Though you weren't a party man,
A Communist you were.
Lenin died so long ago,
And many since have gone.
It's your turn now, Andriusha,
With them to journey on.
The warmth had gone from your skin,
When we kissed your dead forehead.
High above we carried your coffin,
A weight wrapped round in red.
I nailed down the wooden lid,
Little axe-head in tow.
Andrei, how I loved you
Perhaps you'll never know.
No more to-ing and fro-ing,
Along the railway line.
And no more watching the earth
Awake to the dawn sunshine.
You fell before you got there,
Your lips no more will say.
Your grandchildren won't hear you

Sing "little train, away!"
Mother Russia does not mourn,
All those who in her die.
All her devoted children,
Cannot satisfy . . .'

Ivan Vesyolykh suddenly broke down and threw himself from the table towards the door, stepping on the feet of the seated guests and knocking plates on to the floor. No one restrained him.

'Eh, what was he reading?' said one of the noiseless old women disapprovingly, having sat down at the table herself for the last shift. 'It's hard enough for people as it is. And then he goes and makes it worse. It makes your heart ache even more than it does already.'

The widow did not burst into tears, but defended Ivan Vesyolykh:

'He feels guilty though he has done no wrong. Look how he is tormenting himself, while many who are to blame for something don't show their grief by writing poetry, but just sprawl on their guilt, as they would in a soft armchair.'

An engine-driver who had reached Berlin with Andrei Ivanovich thumped at the keys of an accordion – a war trophy that had long since got out of the Lily Marlene habit.

'On the twenty-second of June,
Exactly the clock struck four,
Kiev was bombed, all were informed,
That we had gone to war.'

Everyone began to sing. The widow sang too,

remembering how Andrei Ivanovich had kissed her for the first time after the film *If War Breaks Out Tomorrow*. Then she asked her youngest son:

'You still don't have any children?'

'Still no children.'

'It's about time,' she said. 'And will you be coming to bury me?'

'Mama, what are you saying?' he asked reprovingly, in a tight voice.

'It won't be long now,' she said. 'My legs won't walk at all now. I'd like to rock a child of yours on my foot while my legs have still got a bit of movement in them.' And she called out to the engine-driver with the accordion: 'Hey, play us *Dark Night*. At Andrei Ivanovich's request!'

The youngest Ardabiev saw that the little photographer had got very drunk. He was moving with difficulty towards the door, groping his way along the wall. The camera that dangled on his chest grazed the heads of the seated guests.

The youngest son followed him out into the foul, starless night. The photographer was standing next to the pile of logs in the yard, shaking his fist at the sullen sky:

'One day I'll exhibit everything, everything!'

'Shall I help you home?'

'You'd do better to take a photograph of me!' said the photographer, beginning to roar with laughter. 'You know, I've photographed everyone, but no one's taken a picture of me, apart from the one for my passport!'

Ardabiev walked the photographer home, and he went on muttering:

'I haven't taken pictures of field-marshals or famous

actors. But for forty years I've photographed the ordinary working people. They are my field-marshals, they won the war. They are my famous actors, who play out with brilliance their own lives and deaths, even though they sometimes have to contend with talentless directors!'

Three youths in identical black leather zip-up jackets came up to Ardabiev and the photographer, standing by a street lamp.

'Give us a light!' said one of the youths, with long girlish eyelashes and strange lifeless eyes.

'You're a bit young, aren't you?' said Ardabiev, reluctantly handing him the lighted end of his cigarette.

'We're early birds,' answered the youth, and the other two burst out laughing.

A nasty laugh, thought Ardabiev. Could little Vitya turn out like that too, perhaps? And he walked the photographer on a little.

The latter continued:

'When they want to put an artist down they say his work's photography. They're fools! Photography is a great art! The photographer laughs, cries, accuses, fights! But we Russian photographers are like orphans. There's no Union of Art Photographers. There's no museum of photography. There's no film even. They could yet put up a monument to the unknown Russian photographer!'


As they watched the figures of Ardabiev and the photographer moving away, Filosofer said, between his teeth:

'Well, Speckles, here's your chance. That trendy

fellow's got imported jeans on. Brand new ones. Well?'

'Well, what?' said Speckles uncertainly.

'You're talking in that provincial accent again! Remember what Michurin said about jeans! Here's my knuckleduster for you. Push your fingers in the holes. Go on, they won't break. Have you got your metal flail on you, Fantomas?'

'It's always on me,' answered Fantomas gruffly.

'It's old-fashioned but effective, the weapon of the Black Hundreds. You see, one needn't reject everything from the past,' said Filosofer approvingly. 'I'm not a lover of messy dealings though. Blood is unhygienic. Use violence only in the last resort. I think he'll take them off like a lamb. My only fear is that he'll crap in them. We'd have to get them cleaned.'

Standing at his gate, the photographer appealed to Ardabiev and mankind:

'The editor grumbles that people are badly dressed in my photographs. Does he think I decide what they wear, or something? The regional exhibition jury put a cross against my work because, you see, there were too many suffering faces in them. The fact that people suffer in life doesn't worry them. The main thing is that they shouldn't suffer in photographs. A funny kind of humanism! But the art of photography isn't the same thing as putting together a display board of honoured workers. It's a memorial of history, that's what it is! Bulgakov said that manuscripts don't burn. Neither do negatives!' Having made his appeal the photographer suddenly sobered up and added: 'But

96

they get eaten up by time.' He opened the gate half-way and tentatively suggested: 'Perhaps you'd like to see my studio?'

'All right, but I mustn't stop,' agreed Ardabiev.

'When my landlady's cow passed away the old lady gave me her cowshed to work in,' said the photographer, a little embarrassed, taking Ardabiev into the yard.

'The cow passed away,' repeated Ardabiev thoughtfully, out loud.

'Yes, she passed away. What, shouldn't you say it like that?' bristled the photographer.

'That's the only way to say it,' smiled Ardabiev sadly, thinking of Alla the rat.

If the photographer hadn't told him beforehand, he would never have guessed that he was in what used to be a cowshed. To be sure, a lingering smell of straw, manure and milk seemed to permeate the air. But the walls were freshly whitewashed and floorboards had been laid. There was an iron stove, with a flue leading out through the window. Home-made black paper blinds hung on the windows. Negatives floated in a developing tray under a red lamp on the table. But the walls were the most important thing in the studio, covered with photographs of all sizes – a black and white mosaic of the work, joys and suffering of a small but integral part of mankind, the Siberian town of Khairiuzovsk:

A team of boys from the depot who were still without passports, standing in overalls and caps with earflaps under the red flag they had been awarded. On it the slogan 'All for the Front'.

The sad and at the same time curious eyes of some calves, next to the similarly sad and curious eyes of some soldiers, peeping out from the goods trains being used to transport them.

A blind invalid at the market with a guinea-pig which was drawing typewritten 'fortunes' out of a box. This guinea-pig had probably 'passed away' as well.

A sheet spread out on the church porch, covered with engagement rings, silver spoons, earrings and an ugly gold nugget – the collection for the Front.

A Siberian woman carrying a white moon of frozen milk, with a hole in the middle, under her arm.

A painter on tiptoes, sprucing up a small monument to Lenin with silver paint.

A queue tailing out of a food shop and on to the street, and in the open first-floor window above it, a little boy with a violin on his shoulder.

Girls on a dance floor with tiny garlands of sunflower seeds trailing from their protuberant lips. A carpenter with nails in his mouth, halting his hammer over the rib of a new roof, because a dragonfly had alighted on the half-hammered-in nail.

A boy and a girl, lips converging, and in the background between them an old woman sitting on the mound of earth around her house, leaning her chin on her walking-stick.

Another old woman crying over her cow, knocked down by a lorry.

A third old woman, holding out her wrinkled palm to a young gypsy woman baring cunning teeth, to have her fortune told . . .

'Why so many old women?' asked Ardabiev.

'Because I'm an old woman myself,' said the photographer smiling, and he handed Ardabiev a photograph that hadn't been hung up. 'This one's my most recent.'

Ardabiev took in a dark memorial cross, freshly dug into the nursery school sand-pit. There were two miniature bottles in front of it. The nursery school teacher and children with their buckets and spades stood rooted to the spot, speechless.

'What is that cross doing there?' asked Ardabiev, astonished. 'Who dug it into the nursery school garden?'

'No one knows,' said the photographer, shrugging his shoulders. 'People who have forgotten what the cross comes from.'

'What does it come from?'

'Have you forgotten too?' smiled the photographer sadly. 'From the crucifixion.'

Accompanying Ardabiev to the gate, the photographer said:

'For some reason I don't feel like letting you go. Maybe I should walk you home now. Or would you like to stay the night here? In the cowshed studio?'

'No thank you,' answered Ardabiev. 'My mother will be worrying.'

Ardabiev took a few steps and stopped. Not hearing the squeak of the gate, he realized that the photographer was still watching him, although he probably couldn't see him any more as it was pitch dark.

'You know, everything you've done will be exhibited,' said Ardabiev.

'I don't know, I don't know,' came the photographer's voice from the darkness.

'You do know,' said Ardabiev. 'That is why you work.'

He heard the gate squeaking as the photographer closed it, and set off. The wooden pavement creaked under him as it had when he was a child.

Take the train to Irkutsk in the morning, and from there the first plane to Moscow, thought Ardabiev. I must get a structural analysis of Ardabiola done fast. If only there were a chemical substitute! But if there isn't one? If there isn't one, then plantations of Ardabiola.

Ardabiev winced in hostility when the same youth as before rose up out of the darkness in front of him again.

'That cigarette didn't light up too well, mister,' said the youth, smiling coldly. In his hand was a pistol, which he pointed at Ardabiev's stomach. 'The nice gentleman doesn't want to give a modest friend of mine his pair of jeans, does he? Surely the nice gentleman supports the humane treatment of Soviet children?' he jeered.

'How do you want me to give them to you – with the belt or without?' asked Ardabiev, trying to win time.

He had heard something of similar stories, taking place, he thought, in the Black Sea resort towns. But here, in his native Khairiuzovsk, until recently the home of his father? What a foolish way to die. But he could not risk Ardabiola for the sake of a pair of jeans.

The youth's nerves were breaking and the pistol began to dance in his hands.

'Take off your jeans, you animal!' he shouted hysterically.

'Thanks for the compliment,' said Ardabiev, undoing the jeans and taking off the belt. 'I've always thought the word "animal" had a proud ring to it. Incidentally, I used to have a rat friend for whom I had more respect than I have for many people.'

The pistol suddenly fell out of the youth's shaking

hands and on to the wooden pavement, and Ardabiev heard a tap that had no weight to it at all. The youth grabbed the pistol and again pointed it at Ardabiev.

'Your pistol's a toy one,' said Ardabiev sarcastically. 'While this belt of mine's real. You deserve a good thrashing, and you're going to get one.'

'It's not a toy one!' squealed the youth.

'Yes, it is,' said Ardabiev calmly, moving towards him with his belt raised. 'And you're a toy. A little toy fascist.'

And he lashed him, first on his arms and then right across his face.

'Hit him, Speckles!' shouted the youth with a desperate cry, squeezing himself against the fence.

But Speckles, who had been standing unnoticed behind Ardabiev's back, was unable to lift the hand with the knuckleduster, which suddenly seemed terribly heavy. Then Fantomas sprang and landed an exact Black Hundreds blow with the flail on the back of Ardabiev's head. Past Ardabiev's eyes flashed three still quite boyish faces, distorted by fear and spite . . . then for some reason the wood-shaving-like curls of little Vitya . . . then the girl in the cap on the back platform of the tram . . . then the branch of Ardabiola under the beautiful suede shoes with white stitching. Ardabiev fell with his hands on the fence and began to slip slowly down it.

'Speckles, you scum, hit him!' gasped Filosofer, and he brushed him on the cheekbone with what turned out to be a lighter, made to look like a revolver.

Speckles jumped on top of the fallen Ardabiev and began pounding him on the head with the knuckleduster.

'Now, turn him over to me!' ordered Filosofer.

101

Speckles and Fantomas rolled Ardabiev over so that his face was uppermost. Filosofer sat astride Ardabiev's chest, tore his shirt open and struck him with the revolver-lighter.

'So you said this revolver was a toy?' And he put a little tongue of flame to Ardabiev's nipple.

Ardabiev started and let out a moan. For a moment he opened his eyes: dangling on a chain before his face was an Orthodox cross, which had fallen through the open black leather jacket. Speckles and Fantomas exchanged glances in horror.

'So you said I was a toy? A fascist? There you are, you needn't reject everything from the past,' muttered Filosofer, seemingly intoxicated and running the little tongue of flame over Ardabiev's chest.

'Let's get out of here!' said Speckles, beginning to pull Fantomas by the sleeve.

'Stop, you coward!' said Filosofer, restraining him authoritatively, and Speckles obeyed. 'Take your pair of jeans off him.'

'I don't need the jeans,' said Speckles, his teeth chattering.

'Yes, you do, you need them very badly. You can't live without them, without a pair of real Western jeans,' repeated Filosofer coaxingly. 'Take them off, do as you're told! And you needn't tear his boots off, they're flares. Wait, don't run off! Give it to him in the forehead with the knuckleduster, Speckles, so that his memory fails him for good! Well done! You're making progress before my very eyes! And now let's get out of here.'

They ran past several blocks without meeting a soul in the darkness. Suddenly Speckles began to reel and fell on his knees. He was sick.

'Let me have the jeans,' said Filosofer. 'I want to check the make.' And he flicked the lighter, lighting up the label on the back pocket of the jeans with the flame: 'Lazha . . . ' he said, spitting. 'They're Yugoslav. Sent here to clear. Not from the West at all.'

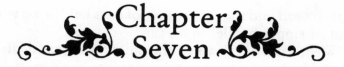

# Chapter Seven

A tiny old woman with beady eyes walked along the canal bank. With one hand she grasped a light sack, from which no clinking sound came, because it held only an empty bottle of Kuban bitter which had nothing to knock against. The old woman turned the yellow autumn leaves over with her stick, but there were no bottles among them. There were none because it had turned cold and the civilized relaxation on the grass with cold food and drinks had ceased. The old woman remembered that there were still the football matches, and that she could switch completely to the Lenin Stadium. The Olympic Games were over now and the entrance to it was open. There were always a lot of bottles there under the stands. However it took a long time to get there and it was far away from her usual deposit counter which would let her jump the queue if she took ten rather than twelve kopecks for each bottle.

'Good morning,' said a voice.

The old woman looked up and saw in front of her a girl wearing a cap.

'Don't you remember me?' asked the girl.

The old woman looked at her suspiciously.

'No,' she replied.

'I came here a month ago,' said the girl in the cap. 'I sat here on this sand dune with a man. His head was shaved bare. Next to us was an orange car, full of bottles. You picked up an empty champagne bottle and asked if you could have it. Then the man with the shaved head said that in a couple of days he'd bring you a lot of empty bottles in his car.'

'Well, what of it?' asked the old woman guardedly.

'Did he bring you empty bottles like he promised?'

'Anyone can make a promise,' scoffed the old woman. 'He promised that in front of you, he was showing off. And then he forgot, and that was that. He would have handed the bottles in himself unless he's a fool.'

'I'm sorry,' said the girl in the cap, and walked away with fast, if not – after her hospital stay – completely steady steps.

The girl in the cap felt that something must have happened to the man with the shaved head if he hadn't brought along the empty bottles as he had said he would. The girl in the cap wanted to see him, but why, she couldn't even have explained to herself.

His surname was all she could remember. At the inquiries bureau they hadn't initially wanted to give her any information without the first name and patronymic. The girl in the cap had pleaded with them. Fortunately it turned out there weren't many Ardabievs in Moscow, and there was only one approaching his age.

The girl found his block and pressed long and hard on the doorbell to the seventh-floor flat, but no one answered.

She came out of the entrance to the block and looked around. There wasn't anyone in the yard, apart from four men playing dominoes under a wooden mushroom meant for children. For some reason one of them was wearing a pair of women's pompom slippers.

The girl went up to the table and asked them:

'Excuse me, do any of you know Ardabiev?'

'How can we know everyone?' muttered the man in pompom slippers. 'It's not like it used to be in the communal flats. Nowadays everyone hides in their flats as if they were burrows. I've been living here four years myself, but I don't know the name of my neighbour across the stairs. Now in our group here we know each other. Dominoes brought us together, you see. Anyway, what's he like, this Ardabiev?'

'His head's shaved. He's got an orange car. He lived on the seventh floor, flat 416. I rang the doorbell but no one answered. And I've absolutely got to see him.'

'Ah, that fellow with the shaved head!' said the man with the pompoms, livening up. 'Of course, of course. I helped him unload his car a month ago. We even had a little drink together, a companionable fellow. And then from that day on he disappeared somewhere. It's true his wife did come round once in his car and put it in the garage. They don't live Russian-style somehow; it's hard to make out whether they live together or apart. But he certainly has disappeared into thin air. Maybe you'd like me to give him a message when he appears?'

'No. There's no need to give him a message,' said the girl in the cap, turning round and walking away.

But scarcely had the man with the pompoms sat down again at the table under the wooden mushroom, happily feeling the dominoes between his fingers, than a piece of notepaper, folded in four, arrived on the table in front of him.

'I've changed my mind,' said the girl. 'Could you give him this, please?'

A day later she was seated on a plane bound for Norilsk, where she had been assigned after graduating from the Institute of Librarianship. Straight away she had to take off her cap and put on one with earflaps, as it had already started snowing in Norilsk. When a reader handed in a book by Glemzer, *Man Against Cancer*, she asked him:

'Would you mind telling me why you took this book out?'

'Not out of curiosity, unfortunately,' he answered. 'I'm a cancer specialist.'

'Have you ever heard of an anti-cancer drug called Ardabiola?'

'No,' he answered, 'I haven't.'

# Chapter Eight

On a lovely morning in September 1981, Ardabiev stood in the yard and washed his car, dipping a cloth into a plastic bucket. This was no longer the orange estate, but a brand new claret-coloured Volga, which he had bought for special foreign trade coupons after his thesis on *The Use of Music in Growing Vegetables* had been issued as a book in Moscow and then republished in the USA, West Germany, France, Italy and other countries which paid hard currency.

The psychology of plants – a mysterious field, as yet little researched. For a long time people have noticed that flowers do badly in homes where there are often family arguments. Transmitters vibrate when approached by a saw or an axe. Ardabiev played music to tomatoes in experimental beds by attaching tape recorder earphones to them – and they began to grow at lightning speed. Several of them reached a kilogram in weight. At first people made fun of Ardabiev. Then they stopped. But surprisingly the tomatoes in their earphones turned out to mean very little to him. The main thing was Ardabiola. While he was growing it at home, in the ordinary boxes of earth, he turned a tape-recorder on at low speed to play recordings of the symphonies, and it too grew more quickly.

Light music did not affect Ardabiola, unlike the hothouse cucumbers which ripened well to the songs of Muslim Magomaev, Yosif Kobzon and Lev Leshchenko. Ardabiola liked Mozart, Beethoven and Tchaikovsky. But Ardabiev's dissertation was not about Ardabiola but the capacity of plants to appreciate music. The value of vegetables to society was obvious. Public recognition of his degree and book came in the material form of the claret-coloured Volga which he was washing in the yard of his block – for the meanwhile he was still in Chertanovo.

Once he had washed the Volga, Ardabiev began screwing an aluminium roof-rack to it. He and his wife were getting ready to go to the South.

This was the first trip Ardabiev had made after flying a year ago to his father's funeral in Khairiu-zovsk, where he had been brutally beaten up and his jeans had been stolen after the funeral dinner. He had needed twelve stitches in his mutilated head. But in a year his hair had grown out, hiding the scars beneath. All that remained was a noticeable dent slightly above the bridge of his nose, and purple burn marks near his nipple.

Everyone had noticed that Ardabiev had changed considerably and, some felt, for the better. Gone was his usual absent-mindedness, when he only half-listened to someone while thinking about something else. He had become attentive to people – especially to the authorities, it was said maliciously. He gladly took part in all the student hops and parties and even played 'Seigneur Tomato' at the children's matinee put on by the institute, as well as going on group outings to ski or pick mushrooms.

He was installing televisions in the experimental seed-beds now, rather than tape recorders, and rumour had it he was working on a doctorate entitled *The Effect of Television on the Growth of Certain*

*Types of Vegetable.* It was impossible to tear him away from the television, especially during hockey matches or the holiday variety show. He had made it up with his wife, and the Mishechkins, whom he couldn't bear before, had become his best friends.

It was with the Mishechkins, no less, that Ardabiev and his wife were about to go to the South, in their two cars.

As he wiped a chamois over the gleaming sides of the Volga, Ardabiev noticed a freshly scratched question mark on her left wing.

'What the hell?' he burst out. 'Who could have done that?'

'Children,' said a hoarse voice next to him. 'Our splendid Soviet children.'

Ardabiev turned and saw a man in women's pompom slippers. The man ran a yellow, nicotine-stained finger over the question mark, examining the quality of the work.

'They used a nail,' he determined.

'But why a question mark in particular?' asked Ardabiev, choking in indignation.

'Would it have been any easier for you if it had been an exclamation mark?' smiled the man with the pompoms. 'There are lots of them around but no one feels any easier because of them.'

'What on earth do I do now?' asked Ardabiev, dropping his arms helplessly. 'We're setting off for the South for a month tomorrow morning, and to bowl along through the entire Soviet Union with a question mark on the side of the car, that's rather, you know . . .' and he couldn't find the words.

The man with the pompoms shared, and even exacerbated, Ardabiev's unease:

111

'I'd say that the traffic police might even be interested, and not without reason. After all, it's a sign of doubt. And doubt about what?'

'And it's not a small one either, it strikes you right in the eye,' said Ardabiev fretfully.

'No, it's not small!' said the man with the pompoms, shaking his head despondently, and he leant towards Ardabiev conspiratorially:

'There are people.'

'There are what?' said Ardabiev, not catching his words.

'Not *what*, but *who*. There are people, I said. They'll do it. They'll do it well. The question mark will be eradicated both in mind and deed.'

'Where are these people?' asked Ardabiev distrustfully.

'Here,' whispered the man with the pompoms, so that no one would be able to hear. 'These people are me.'

'How much?' asked Ardabiev, unintentionally falling into his furtive tone of voice.

'Seeing as how we're neighbours, twenty-five roubles. Righty-ho?' said the man with the pompoms in jocular tone.

'Right,' sighed Ardabiev mirthlessly.

'You provide the right brand of paint and the polish. I'll provide the tool.' And the man with the pompoms took a used match out of a box with a portrait of Tsiolkovsky* on it.

Then with the elegance of a conjuror he dipped the match into the tin of paint that Ardabiev had

---

* Tsiolkovsky, Russian astronomer and inventor, 1857–1935

obligingly brought him, and delicately traced it over the question mark.

'I have an apology to make to you while it dries out. I should have passed a note on to you, but I wasn't able to. First of all you were away, then I was. I was assigned, so to speak, to strengthen the work front at Pereslavl-Zalessky. So I've had the note floating around for almost a year. A girl wrote it.'

'But surely it's been more than a year?' thought Ardabiev. It had been only twelve months since his father had died. But why didn't he remember his father's funeral? It was as if it had happened long, long ago, in another life.

'What was the girl like?' asked Ardabiev absent-mindedly.

'She was wearing a cap,' said the man with the pompoms, looking at him intently. 'An ordinary man's cap. A woolly one, like my mate Venka wears.'

But not the slightest glimmer of interest came into Ardabiev's eyes, and he didn't even ask where the note was. He's being crafty, thought the man with the pompoms. Yes, so that he seems like us, ordinary-like. He's been playing around, most likely, but now he's had to back out. And he asked cheerfully:

'Shall we get on with the polishing?'

'Yes,' agreed Ardabiev despairingly.

The man with the pompoms dabbed some polish on the wing of the Volga and, wheezing, began to spread it with a rag. Having wheezed for about five minutes he drew back his hand with the gesture of a painter admiring his canvas.

The question mark had disappeared.

'That's twenty-five roubles you owe me,' reminded the man in pompom slippers with a quiet dignity.

'But all in all that was fifteen minutes' work,' said Ardabiev flabbergasted, but taking out his wallet.

'But fifteen minutes is a whole lifetime, as Michelangelo said,' asserted the man with the pompoms, tactfully putting him straight. Having got his twenty-five roubles he offered cheerfully:

'In case you need anything I'm always at hand. Under this mushroom in summer and in the recreation room in winter.'

And with his dignity intact he went off home, through the next-door entrance, because there was still some time to go until the hallowed hour of eleven o'clock in the morning.

Before diving into the entrance, however, he took a nail out of the matchbox with the picture of Tsiolkovsky on it, glanced round, and in an instant scratched a new question mark on the wing of someone's gleaming Niva. The man with the pompoms wanted to be of use to mankind.

Ardabiev took one more look at the wing of his car, but there was no question mark on it. It seemed as if the man with the pompoms had carried it away under his arm.

Maybe all that just seemed to happen, thought Ardabiev. The question mark, and that match with the paint on it, and those pompoms too. But my father's funeral, that did happen, only I don't remember it. I know I was beaten up afterwards and my jeans were stolen. But I don't remember how that happened either.

Ardabiev went into his flat and stumbled over the suitcase as he dashed to the telephone which was ringing on the coffee table. Talking was easier than thinking.

114

'Yes, it's me,' said Ardabiev, and suddenly he was needled by a thought – what if it's not me? However, he crushed this idea inside him, flooding it with inconsistently businesslike words: 'Yes, yes, I've filled the tank right up and I'm taking two cans of petrol . . . I've got three lots of smoked sausage . . . At the motel on the Warsaw Road at ten, as we said.' As he put down the receiver, trying to appear purposefully preoccupied, Ardabiev warned his wife: 'The Mishechkins are all ready.'

'The Mishechkins were ready even before they were born,' said his wife, lighting a cigarette and sitting down on the sofa, as if she wasn't planning to go anywhere. 'You never liked the Mishechkins like this before. But now you're thick as thieves with them. Something's happened to you, Ardabiev.' His wife stretched her hand out and stroked the brittle leaves of a plant that protruded from a wooden box. 'Something's happened to you,' she repeated slowly. 'I quarrelled with you over this plant. Over your rat Alla. But when you came out of hospital and mended the cage which Alla the rat had gnawed through, and put a little green parrot in it instead, I didn't know what to think.'

'We never had a rat called Alla! How many times are you going to tell me that story! What are you inventing things for?' exclaimed Ardabiev at the end of his tether. 'What rat?'

'The one that passed away,' said his wife, looking at him searchingly.

'Rats don't pass away, they die,' said Ardabiev, getting his flippers and underwater mask from the cupboard.

'You talked differently before,' said his wife,

continuing to stroke the leaves. 'I was annoyed by the rat and this bush because you spent your time on them and didn't take any notice of me. But you needed them for something. For something you wouldn't discuss with me. I was jealous of your attachment to them. But when you came back you didn't even go up to this wooden box. If I hadn't watered it the bush would have died long ago. And now little fruit have appeared on it again. What did you need those fruit for, Ardabiev?'

'I don't know what the plant's even called. You probably brought it here yourself. Something's happened to your memory,' said Ardabiev, frowning and tucking the flippers and mask into a suitcase.

'No, it's *your* memory that something's happened to. I didn't bring this plant here, Ardabiev. And neither did you. You just got the wooden box and the earth. The bush pushed itself up. When the first tiny leaves appeared on it you clapped your hands like a little boy. Why? Try and remember.' She got up from the sofa and put her hands on his shoulders, peering into his eyes.

'You're tired,' said Ardabiev, kissing her cheek. 'We'll arrive in the South and lie on our backs right next to the sea, and we won't have to think of anything all day long.'

'You never used to be able to do that. You've forgotten how you used to think,' said his wife, nestling up to him and stroking his short brush of hair with her hand, as if trying to jog his memory. Wanting to cause him pain which might make him remember what he had forgotten, and suffering from her own cruelty, she said to him:

'Your scars are under my hand. You were beaten

116

about the head with a knuckleduster and a brick, so that your jeans could be stolen. You had twelve injuries to your skull. You came to in your underpants on the wooden pavement, and set off on your hands and knees for your father's house. You managed to get there. Your brother gave you stitches. I flew to you in the Khairiuzovsk hospital. At first you didn't recognize anyone. Then you recognized your mother. Then me. But when I burst into tears and asked you to forgive me for killing your child, you asked me, "What child?" I was glad that you had forgotten that. But you had forgotten a great many other things as well. You had forgotten what had happened to you. Did those louts really beat your memory out of you? That's what happened to Landau after his car accident. He went on thinking, but stopped being a genius. He suffered from an absurd twist of fate, but those louts had an aim – your jeans. How terrible it would have been if there had been jeans in Pushkin's time, and similar louts had beaten Pushkin's memory out of him. For a wretched pair of jeans.'

'But I'm not Pushkin,' said Ardabiev, joking gloomily in reply.

'Everyone is Pushkin,' said his wife, refusing to give up. 'But you can beat the Pushkin-like qualities out of people. Not just with a knuckleduster, but with education, lying words, indifference. You can make someone forget how they used to think. You can beat the poetry, music and great discoveries out of people. But not everyone gives in. Don't give in, Ardabiev! Try and remember!'

'So aren't tomatoes in earphones a great discovery? What about aubergines contemplating the holiday

117

variety show?' said Ardabiev dejectedly, and suddenly he saw before him the long, girlish eyelashes and frightening lifeless eyes of the youth jabbing him in the stomach with a lighter in the shape of a revolver. 'Take off your jeans, you animal!'

'Ardabiev, touch these leaves – maybe you'll remember what the plant is,' implored his wife, catching hold of him and not letting him get to the suitcases.

'Well, I'm touching them. They're dusty,' said Ardabiev, reluctantly fingering the plant, and all of a sudden he felt as if he were back in the cowshed, with its walls covered in photographs.

The team of boys from the depot stood under the red flag they had been awarded, with the slogan 'All for the Front'.

'They could yet put up a monument to the unknown Russian photographer!' cried the local photographer with the small bluish nose.

'That's not true. I wipe them every morning. Ardabiev, surely you noticed how the leaves quivered when you went near them?' asked his wife, glancing intensely from him to the plant.

'I didn't notice,' answered Ardabiev, but he was lying.

Ivan Vesyolykh recited:

> 'Lenin died so long ago,
> And many since have gone.
> It's your turn now, Andriusha,
> With them to journey on.'

'Once when I put on a record of Britten's Requiem, I caught sight of the bush beginning to move,' continued his wife. 'It was listening. The bush was thinking. It seemed to be burying itself in the Requiem.'

'My work on the sensitivity of vegetables to music has reduced you to mysticism,' said Ardabiev miserably. 'It's time to go. The Mishechkins will already have left.'

He walked towards the suitcases, but his way was barred by the little boy Vitya. He was eating a bar of soap. Then the child vanished.

The man in women's slippers with pompoms walked in through the open door. He hesitated, looking at Ardabiev's wife out of the corner of his eye.

'Well, what kind of message has this mysterious cap-sporting stranger left for us?' said Ardabiev, trying to smile, as if to let the man with the pompoms know that he, Ardabiev, had no secrets from his wife.

The man handed Ardabiev a folded piece of notepaper and went out, backwards for some reason.

Ardabiev unfolded it and showed it to his wife.

'Some kind of nonsense. Someone's playing a practical joke.'

Written on the piece of paper, in large, childish handwriting were the words 'How is your Ardabiola?'

'A father dies only once in a lifetime,' said the captain with little cannons on his collar tabs.

Ardabiev crumpled up the piece of paper and threw it on the floor.

'It's probably one of my students playing a trick on me, taking revenge for an exam he's failed. It's all right, Zosia will clear up. Where is she by the way? We ought to leave her the keys.'

'I'm here,' said Zosia, appearing as if from nowhere. 'Are you going away for long?' She had the beady eyes of the old woman who gathered empty bottles by the canal.

'For three weeks,' answered Ardabiev's wife. 'Could you throw out the rubbish first of all, then wash the floor? Basically tidy it up, please.'

'I can see that needs doing,' said Zosia crossly.

'Here's the parrot feed. His cage needs cleaning out every other day,' continued Ardabiev's wife.

'And what do I do with the parrot while I'm doing that?' asked Zosia suspiciously.

'He's very well-behaved. He'll fly about the room and then get back in the cage of his own accord,' said Ardabiev's wife, reassuring her. 'And water the bush every day . . .'

'And what kind of a bush is that?' asked Zosia. 'Just look at it! It's got berries on it, as well.'

No answer came, either from Ardabiev or his wife, and she understood that this was not a matter for her mind.

While his wife was shutting the suitcase, Ardabiev told Zosia in a low voice:

'Don't water that bush.'

'What are you on about?' asked Zosia, dumbfounded. 'It'll die.'

'Well let it die then. I'm fed up with it!' said Ardabiev, hastening to explain.

'But the mistress . . .' stammered Zosia.

'The mistress is the mistress, but I'm the master here,' whispered Ardabiev quickly, and Zosia sighed, realizing that she was an innocent victim being drawn into an unhappy family matter.

When Ardabiev and his wife had gone into the lift with their suitcases, Zosia, left alone in the flat, began to sweep the floor with a twig broom, stopping in

120

front of the bush in the wooden box.

'Just try and work that one out,' muttered Zosia, 'the mistress says water it, the master says not to. What have families come to!'

Then suddenly she froze, paralysed with fear.

The bush had gently begun to sway and its leaves to rustle.

Zosia looked around: the door and all the windows were closed, and a draught was out of the question. In horror she realized that the bush hadn't been caught by a gust of air, but was swaying of its own accord. She flattened herself against the wall and would have crossed herself, but both her hands were full – one with the broom, the other with the dustpan.

My father has left me, thought Ardabiola sadly, having heard the conversation. My father has ordered that woman not to give me any water. He doesn't even remember what my name is. My father has forgotten that I am his daughter.

Having mustered all her strength, Ardabiola began to swing herself more and more vigorously. She pulled her main root out of the earth and leant against the edge of the wooden box. Then she tensed up to pull out her other roots, both large and small, but in such a way as not to hurt them.

Awkwardly Ardabiola crawled over the edge of the box and on to the floor, and with the uncertain steps of a child learning to walk, went to the window, leaving little clods of earth behind her. She clambered on to the coffee table, whisking off the telephone, and then climbed on to the window-sill. Pressing her branches against the glass, Ardabiola saw her father, sitting in his car and leaving his daughter for ever. Furiously shaking her branches, Ardabiola smashed

121

her entire body against the window and flew downwards, feeling a sharp pain from the splinters of glass.

Ardabiev had already turned on the ignition and was moving off, when the bush crashed on to the bonnet, covering the windscreen with her branches. He slammed on the brakes.

The quivering leaves looked at him through the window and the little green fruit tapped against the glass, as if they wanted to knock right through to him.

'So you told Zosia to throw it out!' cried Ardabiev's wife, and she burst into tears, upset both for herself and for the plant, whose name she did not know.

The green fruit were no longer tapping now, but desperately rattling against the glass, and the branches kept on scratching, as if trying to break into speech.

Ardabiev gripped the wheel and said nothing.

Suddenly he saw two tiny railway workers carrying a minute red coffin lid along one of the branches, without weighing it down. The workers' heads were hidden by the coffin lid, and it was impossible to make out if they were crying or not beneath it.

The little green fruit accompanied the coffin with a drumming beat.

'Show some sense!' cried the stewardess with the boxer-like face.

But another thing that Ardabiev saw through the branches pressing themselves against the glass was the back platform of a tram, and through the window the face of a girl in a cap, which then turned into the face of a thin young Pioneer with troubled, inquiring eyes.

'Will you be coming to bury me?' asked his mother's voice.

'We're not going anywhere,' said Ardabiev to his wife. 'I've remembered everything. It's all come back to me. This bush is Ardabiola.'